U0079386

Good morning
morning
很生活的英語

Let's speak in English ➡

張瑜凌＠編著

● ● ● ● ● ● ● ● ● ● ● ● ●

學英文，實用最重要！

有沒有這樣的經驗：學了十幾年的英文，等到真的需要開口說英文時，卻連一句話也說不了，甚至結結巴巴不知道應該要如何開口說英文？

為什麼會有這樣的現象呢？這是因為台灣的英文教育幾乎都是以「考試」為教學目的，從來不考慮如此填鴨式教育的英文教學方式，是否能造就學子開口說英文的實力，因此台灣學子的英文能力永遠停留在只會看、讀，卻無法開口說的窘境。

如此一來，學到的永遠不是適合一般生活情境所需要用到的英文。

本書「Good morning很生活的英語」特別針對此一現象，編撰了一系列相關生活實用、簡單、易學的英文例句，藉由例句及實用會話的

練習，你可以輕輕鬆鬆地瞭解，在不同情境下，可以使用的相關或類似的說法，只要您能記住其中一句英文，就可以輕鬆用英文溝通。

在一般美國的生活中，並不會使用太艱澀的英文，您只要具備基本的英文字彙基礎，就可以在所有的情境會話中運用自如，舉例來說，"How are you doing?" 是什麼意思？每個單字你都應該認識，但是中文意思呢？其實，英文學習不必逐字翻譯，你只要知道，這是一句問候的語句，表示「你好嗎？」就可以。只要習慣這樣的用法，你自然可以順口說英文。

實用、順口最重要，每天一句，就可以讓你成為說英文的高手！

CONTENTS

Good morning 很生活的英語

問 候

•問句••••••••••••••••••••••

⯈How do you do?
你好嗎？（初次見面用語）

⯈How are you?
你好嗎？

⯈How are you today?
你今天好嗎？

⯈How are you this morning?
今早好嗎？

⯈How are you, Mr. Jones?
瓊斯先生，你好嗎？

⯈How are you doing?
你好嗎？

⯈How are things?
一切都好吧？

⯈How is everything?
最近還好嗎？

⯈How have you been?
你近來好嗎？

⇨How has it been going?
近來好嗎？

⇨How are you getting on?
你怎麼樣？

⇨How was your day?
你今天過得如何？

⇨How was your week?
你這個星期過得如何？

⇨How is your wife?
你的太太好嗎？

⇨How is your family?
你的家人好嗎？

⇨How is everyone?
人家都過得好嗎？

⇨How is your work?
工作進展得如何了？

⇨How is school?
今天在學校過得如何？

⇨Is everything all right?
事情還順利吧？

•回答•••••••••••••••••••••••••••

⇨Fine, thank you.
好,謝謝。

⇨Just fine. Thanks.
還好,謝謝。

⇨Very well. How about you?
很好。你怎麼樣?

⇨All right. And you?
還不錯。你呢?

⇨Great.
很好。

⇨Not bad.
不錯。

⇨O. K.
好。

⇨Pretty good.
很好。

⇨I am great.
我很好。

▷I am all right.
  我很好。

▷I am doing good.
  我很好。

▷Just fine.
  還不錯！

▷I am fine, thank you. How about you?
  我很好，謝謝你。你好嗎？

▷It's going pretty well.
  很順利。

▷Still the same.
  還是一樣。

▷Same as always.
  老樣子。

▷Same as usual.
  和平常一樣。

▷Everyone is fine, thank you.
  每一個人都很好。謝謝你！

▷Not so good.
  沒有那麼好。

➪So so.
　馬馬虎虎。

➪It's terrible.
　很糟糕。

➪Not too well. I have a cold.
　不太好。我感冒了。

➪It's a hard time for for us.
　對我們而言是一段難熬的日子。

實·用·會·話 1

A：Hi! How are you?

B：Fine, thanks. And you?

A：Just fine. Nice weather, isn't it?

B：Yes, we've got a warm day.

A：Are you going somewhere?

B：Downtown.

A：OK. I'll see you later.

B：Good-bye.

A：嗨！你好嗎？

B：不錯，謝了。你呢？

A：還好。天氣很好，不是嗎？

B：是啊，今天暖和。

Λ：你要去什麼地方嗎？

B：去市中心。

A：再見囉！

B：再見！

 深入分析

1. 歐美人士見面喜歡談論天氣，因為這不涉及個人的隱私，因此，假如外國友人向你說 "It's nice today, isn't it?" 你也不必當真，只要回答 "Yes, isn't it?" 即可，其實這也不算什麼回答，說是回應更好，因為天氣好壞任誰都看得出來。他只不過想和你聊一聊以示友好而已。

2. We've got a warm day. 這裏的 have got = have。如：

☑ He's got a temperature.

他發燒了。

實·用·會·話 2

A：Hello. How are you?

B：Fine, thank you. How about you?

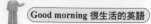

A：Not bad, thanks. Oh, excuse me, here comes my bus. Bye.

B：Bye.

A：嗨！你好嗎？

B：很好，謝謝你。你好嗎？

A：還不錯，謝了。噢，對不起，我的公車來了。再見。

B：再見。

深入分析

　　Here comes my bus. 「我的公車來了。」

　　在英語中，當 there 或 here 放在句首時，通常使用倒裝的語法，例如：

☑There goes the bell.

　　鈴響了。

　　但是，如果主詞是人稱代名詞(he/she/it/they/you)，則不能使用倒裝語法，例如：

☑Here comes Chris. （倒裝句）

　　克里斯來了。

☑Here he comes. （非倒裝句）

　　他來了。

實·用·會·話 3

A：Hello, David, I haven't seen you for a long time!

Where have you been?

B：Hi, it's you, John.

For the past several weeks I was out of town on business matters.

I returned only last Monday.

A：You must come over to my house for dinner.

We have a lot to talk about.

I want to hear all about your trip.

B：It sounds like a good idea.

When is a good time to come?

A：How about next Sunday?

B：That's fine with me. See you Sunday.

A：See you.

A：你好，大衛，很久沒見了！

你跑到那裏去了？

B：嗨，是你啊，約翰。

過去幾週我出差去了。

上週一才回來。

A：你一定要到我家來吃飯。

我們好好聊聊。

我想聽聽你旅途上的事。

B：好主意。

什麼時候去好呢？

A：下個星期天怎樣？

B：我可以。星期天見。

A：再見。

 深入分析

1. It sounds like a good idea. 「聽起來是不錯的主意。」

此句中 it 是形式主詞，sounds like 意思是「聽起來……」，例如：

☑ That sounds nice.

那聽起來倒是不錯。

☑ It sounds OK to me.

對我來說沒有問題。

☑ It sounds terrible.

那聽起來很糟糕。

2. How about…? 「……如何？」

通常用來向別人提出建議，是一種徵詢意見的語句，例如：

☑How about next Sunday?

　下星期天如何？

☑How about going for an outing?

　出去郊遊怎麼樣？

☑How about a cup of coffee?

　來杯咖啡如何？

實·用·會·話 4

A：Hello, Peter.

B：Hi, Joy. How are you doing?

A：Great. How about you? Is everyone OK?

B：Everyone is fine except David.

A：David? What happened to him?

B：He broke his leg in a car accident.

A：I am sorry to hear that. Is it serious?

B：I am not sure. I will call him on tonight.

A：Please send my regards to him.

A：哈囉，彼得。

B：嗨，喬依。你好嗎？

A：不錯，你呢？大家都好嗎？

B：除了大衛之外，大家都不錯。

A：大衛？他怎麼啦？

B：他在一場車禍中摔斷腿了。

A：真是遺憾。嚴重嗎？

B：我也不確定。我今晚要去拜訪他。

A：幫我向他問好。

 深入分析▪▪■▪

> except 表示「除了……之外」，可當介系詞及連接詞使用，例如：
>
> ☑We all go to school except that young girl.
>
> 　除了那位年輕的女孩之外，我們全都去上學。
>
> ☑David did nothing except complain while he was here.
>
> 　大衛在這裡時除了抱怨之外，還是抱怨。

1. Who is closer to you, your mom or your dad?

   爸爸和媽媽誰和你較親密？

2. Can you go to the cinema with your watch broken?

   你手錶壞了，可以去看電影嗎？

3. Why is the comet like Micky Mouse?

   為什麼說彗星像米老鼠？

英語腦筋急轉彎 解答

1. Mom is closer, because dad is farther.

   媽媽較親近，因為爸爸是較遠。

   原來如此

   farther「較遠的」與 father「父親」發音相似。

2. Of course not, for I don't have the time.

   當然不行，因為我沒有時間。

   原來如此

   因為問「現在幾點鐘」是 "What time have you?"，
   但是因為沒有戴錶，所以「沒有時間」。

3. It's a star with a tail.

   因為它是一根帶有尾巴的巨星。

   原來如此

   表示 comet 和米老鼠一樣有尾巴(tail)。

Unit 2

介 紹

●介紹●

○ I don't think you've met each other before.
  我想你們倆以前沒見過面吧！

○ Have you ever met Tom?
  你見過湯姆嗎？

○ Have you ever met my husband?
  你見過我的先生嗎？

○ Do you know that girl in black?
  你認識那位穿黑衣的女孩嗎？

○ Do you know Ruby?
  你認識露比嗎？

○ Let me introduce myself.
  讓我自我介紹。

○ Allow me to introduce Miss Smith.
  請允許我來介紹史密斯小姐。

○ Allow me to introduce you to Mr. Baker.
  請允許我把你介紹給貝克先生。

○ David, let me introduce Mr. Jones to you.
  大衛，我來介紹一下瓊斯先生給你認識。

➪I'd like to introduce my friend Tom.
　我想介紹一下我的朋友湯姆。

➪I'd like you to meet my friend Tom.
　我想讓你來見一下我的朋友湯姆。

➪I'd like you to meet a friend of mine.
　我希望你見見我的一位朋友。

➪I'd like you to meet my family.
　我希望你見見我的家人。

➪I'd like you to meet Mr. Jones, my boss.
　我想要你認識瓊斯先生，我的老闆。

➪Mary, meet my friend Tom.
　瑪麗，來見我的朋友，湯姆。

➪Chris, this is Mr. Jones.
　克里斯，這是瓊斯先生。

➪Sophia, this is Chris. Chris, this is Sophia, my
　sister.
　蘇菲亞，這是克里斯。克里斯，這是我妹妹
　蘇菲亞。

➪Meet Tom.
　來見一下湯姆。

▷Come to meet Tom.
來見見湯姆。

▷I am Tom Jones, David's boss.
我是湯姆·瓊斯，大衛的老闆。

▷She is my wife Sally.
她是我的太太莎莉。

▷They are my parents.
他們是我的父母。

▷I am Sally's sister.
我是莎莉的姐姐。

▷This is Mr. White.
這是懷特先生。

▷They are Mr. and Mrs. Lee.
他們是李先生和李太太。

▷Tom is an old friend of mine.
湯姆是我的一個老朋友。

● 介紹後的打招呼 ● ● ● ● ● ● ● ● ● ● ● ● ● ● ●

▷Hello.
哈囉！

⤷Hello yourself.
你好啊！

⤷Hi, Tom.
嗨，湯姆。

⤷How do you do?
你好。

⤷I'm pleased to meet you.
我很高興認識你。

⤷Glad to meet you.
很高興認識你。

⤷Nice to meet you.
很高興認識你。

⤷Good to meet you.
很高興認識你。

⤷Pleased to meet you.
很高興認識你。

⤷Very nice to meet you.
非常高興認識你。

⤷It's my pleasure to meet you.
認識你是我的榮幸。

⮕Nice to meet you, too.
我也很高興認識你。

⮕I've heard so much about you.
久仰你的大名。

⮕I've heard a lot about you.
久仰大名。

⮕Please call me Tom.
請叫我湯姆。

⮕Just call me Tom.
叫我湯姆就好了。

實·用·會·話 1

A：Oh, I don't think you've met each other before. Mary, meet my friend Tom. Tom, this is Mary.

Mary: Glad to meet you.

Tom: Nice to meet you, too.

Mary: I've heard so much about you.

Tom: Same with me. By the way, how are things going with you?

Mary: Everything is OK . How about you?

Tom: I'm very busy now.

A : Tom is preparing for an examination.

Mary: Good luck with you.

Tom: Thank you very much.

A：哦，我想你們倆以前沒見過吧。瑪麗，來見
　　我的朋友，湯姆。湯姆，這是瑪麗。

瑪麗：很高興認識你。

湯姆：我也很高興認識你。

瑪麗：我已經久仰你的大名了。

湯姆：我也是。順便問一下，你現在好嗎？

瑪麗：一切都好。你呢？

湯姆：現在我很忙。

A：湯姆正在準備考試。

瑪麗：祝你好運。

湯姆：非常感謝。

 深入分析

1. meet 除了是「見面」的意思之外，用在介
　 紹的場合時，中文則翻譯為「認識」，而
　 非使用 "know"，例如：

☑你如何認識你的太太？

How did you know your wife? (誤)

How did you meet your wife? (正)

2. How are things going with you?「你過得
   好嗎？」

   是向人表達關切的話，實際上就相當於
   How are you?的問句。

3. How about you?「你呢？」

   這裏的 "How about…?" 是用來表達關心
   別人的健康情況，而且往往用在別人問完
   "How are you?" 而你回答自己的狀況後
   才反問的問題。

實·用·會·話 2

(A is introducing her new roommate to a
neighbor.)

A：Hi, Lucy. I don't think you've met Peggy.
   Peggy is my new roommate. Peggy, this
   is Lucy. Lucy lives next door.

Peggy: Nice to meet you, Lucy.

Lucy: Nice to meet you, too, Peggy.

(A 正在把新室友介紹給鄰居)

A：你好，露茜。我想你沒見過佩姬吧。佩姬是

我的新室友。佩姬，這是露茜。露茜就住在隔壁。

佩姬：很高興認識你，露茜。

露茜：也很高興認識你，佩姬。

實·用·會·話 3

（A is introducing the guest to the dean of college.）

A：Dean Li, may I present Dr. John Wells, our guest speaker for today, Dr. Wells, this is Dean Li.

Li：How do you do?

John：I'm pleased to meet you.

A：Dean Li will introduce you to the audience today.

John：I'm honored.

Li：It is my pleasure.

（A正在把演講來賓介紹給學院的主任）

A：李主任，我可以介紹今天的演講來賓嗎？約翰・威爾斯博士，這是李主任。

李主任：你好。

約翰：很高興能認識你。

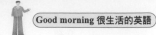

A：李主任將把你介紹給今天的聽眾。

約翰：我很榮幸。

李主任：我很高興這麼做。

 深入分析

H ow do you do?「你好嗎？」

通常用在初次見面時，而且多用於和英國人見面之時。美國人好像更不拘於小節，往往一句 "Hi" 就可達到初次見面的打招呼的目的了。

實·用·會·話 4

A：Hello.

B：Hello youeself.

A：My name is David.

B：I'm Susan.

A：Where are you from?

B：I am from America.

A：Are you in the Chinese language program?

B：Yes. Are you in the program, too?

A：Yes. I'm the Chinese tutor.

大衛：哈囉！

蘇珊：哈囉！

大衛：我的名字叫大衛。

蘇珊：我是蘇珊。

大衛：你從哪兒來？

蘇珊：我來自美國。

大衛：你是選修中文課程的嗎？

蘇珊：是的。你也是修這個課程嗎？

大衛：是的。我是中文輔導教師。

 深入分析

　　Are you in the program, too?「你也選修這門課嗎？」

　　這裏的 "program" 是指教學的計劃或課程，例如：

☑He is in the postgraduate program.

　　他是研究生。

實·用·會·話 5

A：Chris, this is Mr. Brown. This is our monitor, Chris.

B：I'm very happy to see you, Mr. Brown.

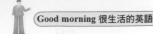

C：It's good to meet you, too.

B：How do you find things over here?

C：It's quite different from what I expected.

B：Don't worry, you'll soon get used to it.

A：克里斯，這是布朗先生。這是我們的班長，克里斯。

B：見到您非常高興，布朗先生。

C：見到你也真好。

B：您覺得這裏怎麼樣？

C：與我所想像的十分不同。

B：別擔心，您不久就會習慣的。

深入分析

1. "be different from" 是一種固定搭配的用法，意思是「與～不同」，如：

☑Your method is different from mine.

你的方法與我的不同。

☑This book is different from that one in color.

這本書與那本書的顏色不同。

2. You'll soon get used to it. 「你會習慣的。」

"get used to" 意思是「變得習慣於～」，這裏的 "to" 是介詞，後面要接名詞、代詞或動名詞，例如：

☑The old woman got used to living alone
after her husband died.

自從丈夫死後，老太太習慣了獨自生活。

☑He hasn't got used to life in Taipei.

他還不習慣台北的生活。

1. What's the largest room in the world?

   世界上最大的房間是什麼房間？

2. What's the poorest bank in the world?

   世界上最沒有錢的銀行是什麼銀行？

3. When is coffee like the surface of the earth?

   咖啡什麼時候像地球表面？

4. What month do soldiers hate?

   當兵的不喜歡幾月份？

1. The room for improvement.

   待改進的空間。

   原來如此

   room 除了是「房間」之外，也表示「空間」的意思。

2. The river bank.

   河堤。

   原來如此

   bank 除了是「銀行」解釋，也可以是「河堤」。

3. When it's ground.

   被碾成粉末時。

   原來如此

   ground 可以作為「地面」及「磨成粉末」。

4. March.

   三月。

   原來如此

   march 代表「三月份」及「軍隊」的意思。

Unit **3**

客套話

➪I am pleased to see you again.
很高興再看見你。

➪Nice to see you again.
很高興再看見你。

➪Nice to see you.
見到你真好。

➪Good to see you again.
好高興又再見到你。

➪I am so happy to see you.
我很高興見到你。

➪Nice weather, isn't it?
天氣很好，不是嗎？

➪Are you going somewhere?
你要去什麼地方嗎？

➪You look great.
你看起來很不錯耶！

➪You look terrible.
你看起來很糟糕！

➪Hey, what's going on here?
嘿，這裡發生什麼事？

▷I have not seen you for a long time.
好久不見了！

▷Long time no see.
好久不見。

▷It has been a long time.
真是好久了。（指時間過得真快）

▷You haven't changed at all.
你一點都沒變。

▷I am sorry to hear that.
我很遺憾聽見這件事。

▷I am glad for you.
我很為你高興。

▷I am proud of you.
我為你感到驕傲。

▷Nice talking to you.
很高興和你說話。

實·用·會·話 1

A：Hi, Maggie.

B：Sophia! Have a seat.

A：Thanks.

B：Nice to see you again.

A：Me too. Do you work around here?

B：Yes, I work at Hyatt Hotel.

A：嗨！瑪姬。

B：蘇菲亞。請坐。

A：謝謝！

B：很高興又見到你。

A：我也是。你在這裡工作嗎？

B：是啊！我在君悅飯店工作。

 深入分析

　　Have a seat. 「請坐。」

　　請人坐下的說法有許多種，Have a seat 是比較隨性的用法，其他的說法還有以下幾種：

☑Take a seat.

　　請坐。

☑Sit down, please.

　　請坐。

☑Sit.

　　坐！

實·用·會·話 2

A：David?

B：Scott! What are you doing here?

A：I visited one of my friends around here.

B：How are you doing?

A：Still the same. And you? You look great.

B：I just got married last week.

A：Congratulations.

B：Thanks.

A：大衛？

B：史考特？你在這裡作什麼？

A：我來附近拜訪一位朋友。

B：你好嗎？

A：老樣子。你呢？你看起來氣色不錯。

B：我上個禮拜結婚了。

A：恭喜。

B：謝謝！

 深入分析

get married「結婚」

結婚的動詞是 marry，相關用法如下：

☑He married Sophia last month.

　他去年和蘇菲亞結婚。

☑They got married in 2003.

　他們是 2003 年結婚的。

實·用·會·話 3

A：Hi, Katy.

B：Oh, hi, David.

A：What's wrong? You look upset.

B：I just got a lay off.

A：I am so sorry to hear that.

B：It's OK. I am looking for a job now.

A：嗨，凱特。

B：噢，嗨，大衛。

A：怎麼啦？你看起來心情不好

B：我被遣散了。

A：我很遺憾聽到這件事。

B：沒關係。我現在正在找工作。

Unit **4**

寒 暄

⇨What a surprise!
多讓人驚奇呀！

⇨What a shame!
多可惜呀！

⇨What a fine day!
多好的天氣呀！

⇨What a coincidence!
多巧啊！

⇨I haven't seen you for ages.
真是好久不見了。

⇨I haven't seen you for a long time.
我有好久沒見你了。

⇨I haven't seen you for months.
好幾個月沒見到你了。

⇨I haven't seen you for weeks.
我有幾個星期沒見你了。

⇨You look beautiful.
你看起來很漂亮。

⇨You look great.
你看起來氣色不錯。

➪You look smart.
你看起來很有精神。

➪You look very happy.
看樣子你很高興。

➪You look a bit tired.
看樣子你有點累了。

➪You look terrible.
你看起來遭透了。

➪You look pale.
你看起來臉色蒼白。

➪What's the hurry?
你在趕什麼？

➪What are you doing here?
你在這裡做什麼？

➪Are you coming alone?
你自己來嗎？

➪Where are you going?
你要去那裡？

➪I've been away on a business trip.
我去出差了。

⇨I've been away on vacation.
　我出去度假了。

⇨I've been away to New York.
　我去了紐約。

⇨I've been away doing shopping.
　我出去買東西了。

實·用·會·話 1

A：Say, aren't you Tony Hudson?

B：Yes. That's right. Do I know you?

A：Didn't you attend the party last night?

B：Yes, but I ...

A：Well, we were introduced before the party. I'm Bob Andrews.

B：Oh, yes! How could I forget!
　　You were with a blond lady then.

A：嘿，你叫湯尼‧哈德遜吧？

B：是的，我們認識嗎？

A：你不是參加了昨晚的聚會了嗎？

B：參加了，但我……

A：呃，我們是聚會之前經介紹認識的。我叫鮑勃·安德魯斯。

B：天哪，我怎麼會忘了呢。你當時是和一位金髮女郎在一起的。

深入分析

> say 是「說話」的意思，在口語化中則是「喂、等等、那個」的意思，有感嘆之意的用語。

實·用·會·話 2

A：Look, who's here, Paul!

B：Hey, Peter. Fancy meeting you here. I thought you were abroad.

A：I just got back. It's nice to see you both here. What a coincidence!

B：We're here on holiday. Tell me how was your trip to America.

A：瞧！誰在這兒，保羅！

B：嘿，彼得！真沒想到在這兒見到你。我以為你出國了。

A：我剛剛回來。在這兒見到你們二位真高興。

多巧啊！

B：我們是來度假的。告訴我你美國之行的情況吧。

 深入分析

1. I thought ... 「我以為……」

   當某事與預期中不相符時使用，後面的子句必須用過去式表示，例如：

   ☑ I thought she was mad at me.

   我以為她在生我的氣。

2. Fancy meeting you here. 「很訝異在這裡遇見你。」

   這裏的 fancy 用於感歎語氣，表示驚訝，例如：

   ☑ Fancy her saying such unkind things about you!

   她竟然說出這些對你無情的話！

   ☑ Just fancy! How strange!

   多奇怪呀！真想不到。

3. What a coincidence! 感歎句，意思是「多麼巧合呀」，多用於巧遇時或發生某件令人不得不相信的巧合之事。

實·用·會·話 3

A: Hello, Jackie! Fancy meeting you here! How are you these days?

B: Fine, just fine. And you?

A: Things couldn't be better. And how's Jim doing?

B: He's the same. You know him, always busy, in the office or at home.

A: Oh, Jim. Look, I'm late for work. I'll phone you some time later, but now I must rush.

B: All right. See you!

A: 你好，傑克！真沒想到在這兒見到你。你近來好嗎？

B: 好，很好。你呢？

A: 非常好。吉姆怎樣？

B: 他還是老樣子。你瞭解他總是很忙的，不是在辦公室忙，就是在家裏忙。

A: 哎，吉姆這傢伙。哦，我上班要遲到了。我再打電話給你，但現在我得趕時間。

B：好的，再見！

 深入分析

1. Things couldn't be better. 「事情再好不過了。」

   couldn't be better 這種否定形式接形容詞的比較級句型常常表示「極端」，這句話的意思是「不能再好了」，例如：

   ☑ The traffic jam couldn't be worse.

   交通阻塞真是糟透了。

2. Look! 「聽我說。」

   這是一種英語口語化的說法，並不是教對方「看」，而是引起對方注意的一種語助詞，例如：

   ☑ Look! Here comes John.

   看，約翰來了。

   ☑ Look! Don't blame yourself. It's not your fault.

   聽著，別責怪你自己。不是你的錯。

實·用·會·話 4

A：I think I've seen you before.

B：No, I don't think so.

A：Aren't you Robert Jones?

I believe we met at a sales conference last summer.

B：Yes. Now I remember.

You're an engineer. What a coincidence!

A：You know what they say. It's a small world.

B：Perfectly right. Ha, ha, ha....

A：我想我曾見過你。

B：不，我想沒見過。

A：你不是叫羅勃特‧瓊斯嗎？

我相信我們是去年夏天在一次銷售會議上認識的。

B：對，我想起來了。

你是一位工程師。真巧啊！

A：你知道人們是怎麼說的：「這世界真小」。

B：完全正確。哈哈哈……!

實‧用‧會‧話 5

A：Hello, Tom.

B：Oh, Mr. White. How have you been?

A : Pretty good, thank you.

B : You look a bit tired.

A : It's nothing. I was up late last night.

B : Well, I have to go. Peter's waiting for me.

A : OK. It's nice seeing you again. Good-bye!

B : Bye!

A：湯姆，你好！

B：噢，懷特先生。你好嗎？

A：很好，謝謝。

B：你看起來有點累。

A：沒事，我昨晚太晚睡了。

B：哎呀，我得走了，彼得在等我。

A：好的，見到你真好。再見！

B：再見！

 深入分析

　　be up late /stay up late 意思是「熬夜（到很晚）」，例如：

☑Children shouldn't stay up late.

　小孩子不應該熬夜。

☑Don't stay up late tonight; you'll have to get up early tomorrow morning.

今晚就別熬夜了，你明天要早起呢！

實·用·會·話 6

A：What a surprise! Meeting you here.

B：I haven't seen you for ages. Where have you been?

A：I've been away on a business trip.

B：Where did you go?

A：Japan.

A：真沒想到，我們在這兒見面了。

B：好久沒見面了，你上哪兒去了？

A：我去出差了。

B：去哪兒出差了？

A：日本。

 深入分析

1. I haven't seen you for ages.「好久沒看見你了！」

  這裏的 for ages = for a long time 表示「很長時間、很久」之意，例如：

☑We've been waiting for ages.

我們已經等候很久了。

2. ages 也可以表示時間很久了，例如：

☑It's ages since I saw you last.

自從上次見到你到現在已經好久了。

想一想，別急著翻到下一頁看答案，
答案可是會出人意料之外喔！

1. Why is the bride unhappy on her wedding day?

   新娘在新婚日為何不開心？

2. What time must it be when the escaped hungry wolf
   ate the paymaster?

   逃跑了的餓狼吃掉出納員是什麼時候？

3. What will you break once you say it?

   什麼東西說出來就碎了？

英語腦筋急轉彎 解答

1. Because she didn't marry the best man.

   因為她沒有嫁給最好的人。

   原來如此

   best man 是「男儐相」，字面意思是「最好的人」
   的意思，而「新郎」是 groom。

2. 8 p.m.

   下午8點。

   原來如此

   8 的發音〔et〕，與 eat 的過去式 ate〔et〕一樣；
   而 pm 則是代表 paymaster 的戲稱。

3. Silence.

   沉默。

   原來如此

   因為「打破沉默」叫做 break silence。

Unit 5

道 別

•說再見• • • • • • • • • • • • • • • • • • • •

⇨Bye-bye.
再見！

⇨Goodbye.
再見！

⇨See you.
再見！

⇨See you later.
待會見。

⇨See you around.
待會見！

⇨See you Sunday.
星期日見！

⇨See you tomorrow.
明天見！

⇨See you next time.
下次見！

⇨I will see you sometime.
下次見！

・暗示要說再見・ ●●●●●●●●●●●●●●●●●●●●

▷I think I should be going.
我想我要走了。

▷I have to go.
我必須走了。

▷I have got to go.
我必須走了。

▷I really have to go.
我真的要走了。

▷I hate to say goodbye.
我討厭說再見。(意思是「真的要走了」)

▷I have come to say goodbye.
我順道來說一聲再見。

▷I would like to say goodbye to everyone.
再見了，各位。

▷Let's go home.
我們回家吧！

▷It's getting late.
時候不早了。

• 約定見面 • •

▷See you at 10 o'clock.
十點鐘見。

▷See you at the lounge.
大廳見。

▷See you again next week.
下星期再見。

▷I hope we meet again soon.
希望我們可很快再見面。

▷Hope to see you soon.
希望能很快地再見到你。

▷I hope we meet again soon.
希望我們不久後能夠盡快再見面。

▷I hope to see you soon again.
希望很快再見到你。

▷I can't wait to see you again.
我等不及再看到你。

▷Let's get together again soon.
我們盡快再找個時間聚一聚。

▷Let's get together sometime.
　有空聚一聚吧！

▷If you're ever in Taipei, you must look me up.
　如果你來台北，一定要來拜訪我。

留下聯絡方式

▷Do you have a cellular phone?
　你有手機嗎？

▷How do I contact you?
　我要如何聯絡你？

▷This is my business card.
　這是我的名片。

▷Here is my e-mail address.
　這是我的電子郵件信箱。

▷Let me write down your phone number.
　我來寫下你的電話號碼。

▷May I have your MSN account?
　可以給我你的MSN帳號嗎？

保持聯絡

▷Give me a call when you're next in town.
　如果下次你進城，打個電話給我。

⇨Call me when you arrive in Taiwan.
到台灣時打個電話給我。

⇨Give me a call sometime.
偶爾給我個電話吧。

⇨Call me sometime.
偶爾打個電話給我吧！

⇨You'll stay in touch, won't you?
你會保持聯絡吧？

⇨Don't forget to keep in touch.
別忘了要保持聯絡。

⇨Let's keep in touch.
保持聯絡。

⇨We'll keep in touch.
我們要保持聯絡！

⇨Don't forget to write.
別忘了寫信（給我）。

⇨Write me sometime.
有空寫信給我。

⇨Meet you on line.
線上再見囉！

▷Please call again any time you like.
隨時都可以打電話給我。

● 祝福用語 ●

▷Good luck.
祝你好運。

▷Good luck to you.
祝你好運。

▷Take care.
保重。

▷Goodbye and have a good trip.
再見，祝你一路順風。

▷Take care of yourself, my friend.
我的朋友，請保重。

▷Take care and goodbye.
保重，再見了。

▷Safe flight.
旅途平安！

▷Safe trip.
旅途平安！

▷Have a good flight back.
祝你回程旅途平安。

▷Have a safe trip.
祝你旅途平安。

▷Have a good trip.
祝你旅途平安。

▷Please say hello to Mr. White for me.
請幫我向懷特先生打招呼。

▷Please give my best regards to your mother.
請幫我向你母親問好。

客套話 ••••••••••••••••••••••••

▷It was really fun hanging out with you.
跟你相處真是有意思。

▷Nice talking to you.
很高興和你聊天。

▷Have a nice day.
祝你有美好的一天。

▷Don't work too hard.
不要工作太累。

⇨Take it easy.

放輕鬆點。

⇨I will miss you.

我會想念你的。

實·用·會·話 1

A：So you will call Mr. Jones, won't you?

B：Yes, I have to.

A：Don't worry about it. It's no big deal.

B：Thanks. I got to go now. Bye.

A：See you.

A：所以你會打電話給瓊斯先生，對吧？

B：是的，我必須要。

A：別擔心，沒什麼大不了的。

B：謝啦！我要走了，再見。

A：再見。

深入分析

　　美國人說「再見」有許多種方式，see you next time 是單純「再見」的意思，並不一定表示兩人已約好下次見面的時間了，所以下次聽

見美國人說 see you next time 時，可別會錯意以為雙方還有約而追問對方：When？（什麼時候）

實·用·會·話 2

A：Is there anything I can do for you, Mr. Jones?

B：No, I can manage it myself.

A：So can I go home now?

B：Sure. Don't worry about me.

A：OK. See you tomorrow.

B：Bye.

A：瓊斯先生，有沒有需要我幫忙的事？

B：沒有，我可以自己處理。

A：所以我可以現在走了嗎？

B：好啊！別擔心我。

A：好的。明天見囉！

B：再見。

實·用·會·話 3

A：Where are you going?

B：Taipei Railway Station.

A：It's on my way home.

B：Can you give me a lift?

A：Sure. Get in.

(Later)

A：Here we are.

B：Thanks. See you later.

A：Bye and take care.

A：你要去哪裡？

B：台北車站。在我回家的路上。

A：你能讓我搭便車去嗎？

B：當然好，上車吧！

（稍後）

A：我們到了。

B：謝啦！再見。

A：拜拜，小心喔！

 深入分析

　　give sb. a lift「讓某人搭便車」

　　lift 表示抬起、舉起之意，而「讓人搭便車」除了 give sb. a lift 之外，相同意思還有 give sb. a ride 的用法。而 give sb. a lift 也有「助人一臂之力」的意思，例如：

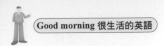

☑Could anybody give me a lift there and back?

有沒有人能送我過去和回來？

☑Can I give you a lift to school?

需要我讓你搭便車上學去嗎？

Unit **6**

問 路

•問句• •

➪I am lost.
　我迷路了。

➪Where am I on the map?
　我在地圖上的哪裡？

➪What street am I on?
　我在哪一條街上？

➪Can I get some directions?
　能問一下路嗎？

➪Excuse me, where is the Museum?
　抱歉，博物館在哪裡？

➪Do you know where the Museum is?
　你知道博物館在哪裡嗎？

➪Where is the nearest gas station?
　最近的加油站在哪裡？

➪Excuse me, could you tell me the way to...?
　請問，你能告訴我去……的路嗎？

➪Excuse me, could you show me the way to...?
　請問，你能指點我去……的路嗎？

➪Excuse me, but where is the...?
請問，……在哪兒？

➪Excuse me, could you tell me how I can get to the...?
請問，你能告訴我怎樣到……嗎？

➪How can I get to...?
我怎樣到……呢？

➪Is this the road to...?
這是去……的路嗎？

➪What's the name of this road?
這條路是什麼路名？

➪Excuse me, does this street lead to...?
請問，這條街通往……嗎？

➪How far from here?
從這裏去有多遠？

➪How long does it take on foot?
走路要多久的時間？

➪Can I walk there?
我可以走路過去嗎？

➪Shall I take a taxi?

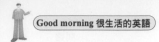

我應該要搭計程車嗎？

⇨Can you direct me to the police office?
你能告訴我去警察局怎麼走嗎？

⇨Would you tell me how to go to Railway Station?
你能告訴我如何去火車站嗎？

⇨Where is the entrance to TICC?
台北國際會議中心的入口在哪裡？

⇨How can I get to this address?
我要怎麼到這個地址？

⇨Are there any landmarks on the way?
路上有沒有任何路標？

⇨Which side of the street is it on?
在街道的哪一邊？

⇨Where can I take a taxi?
我可以在那裡招到計程車？

⇨Where can I buy the ticket?
我要去哪裡買車票？

⇨Which train goes to New York?
哪一班車廂到紐約？

➪Is the right line for New York?
去紐約是這條路線嗎？

➪Is this the right platform for New York?
這是出發到紐約的月台嗎？

➪Where should I transfer to go to New York?
我要到哪裡轉車到紐約？

➪Where should I change trains for New York?
去紐約要去哪裡換車？

➪Where should I get off to go to New York?
到紐約要在哪裡下車？

➪Does this bus go to New York?
這班公車有到紐約嗎？

➪Is this bus stop for New York?
這個站牌有到紐約嗎？

➪Does this bus stop at City Hall?
這班公車有停靠在市政府站嗎？

➪How often does this bus run?
公車多久來一班？

➪How many stops are there to Taipei?
到台北有多少個站？

◇What's the next station?
下一站是哪裡？

◇Which stop is nearest to City Hall?
哪一站最靠近市政府？

◇I missed my stop.
我錯過站了。

● 回答 ●

◇It's on the right.
在右邊。

◇It's on your right.
在你的右手邊。

◇Turn right at the second crossing.
在第二個十字路口向右轉。

◇Turn left when you see the T junction.
看到T形路口，向左轉。

◇Take the second right.
第二個路口向右走。

◇It's the second left.
第二個路口向左轉。

✑Take a number 11 bus and get off at the Zoo.
搭乘11路公共汽車，到動物園下車。

✑It's across from City Hall.
就在市政府對面。

✑It's next to the school.
就在學校旁邊。

✑The post office is just across from the school.
郵局就在學校對面。

✑It's on the opposite of the post office.
就在郵局對面。

✑The school is opposite to the post office.
學校就在郵局的對面。

✑It's between the school and the post office.
就在學校和郵局之間。

✑It's on the right side of the school.
在學校的右邊。

✑It's in front of the school.
就在學校前面。

✑Go straight ahead and then take the first turn
on the left.

一直向前走，然後在第一個路口向左轉。

⇨Go straight for three blocks.
向前走三條街就到了。

⇨Go straight along this street.
沿著這條路走。

⇨Go straight along this street for two blocks.
沿著這條路向前走兩個街道。

⇨Go straight ahead about four blocks and turn left.
直走過四個街段再左轉。

⇨Go straight ahead until you see the traffic light.
直走到紅路燈為止。

⇨Turn right at the second traffic light.
在第二個紅綠燈處右轉。

⇨Turn left and you will see it on your right side.
左轉後，在你的右手邊。

⇨You will see it at the corner on your right.
你會看到在你右手邊的轉角處。

⇨You are here.
你在這裡。

▷You are going the wrong direction.
你走錯方向了。

▷You can get there on foot.
你可以走路去。

▷You'd better take a bus.
你最好搭公車。

▷I'm going there myself. Follow me please.
我正要去那兒。請跟我來。

▷I'll walk you there. It's on my route.
我帶你去那兒。我正好路過那兒。

▷It's about half a mile from here.
離這兒大約半英里。

▷It's not far. Just two blocks away.
不遠。離這兒有兩個街區。

▷It's about ten minutes' walk.
步行大約需要十分鐘。

▷It takes just five minutes' walk.
走路需要五分鐘。

▷It is a five-minute walk.
走路需要五分鐘。

▷It's about ten minutes' ride from here.
　從這兒搭車大約十分鐘。

▷You won't miss it.
　你不會找不著的。

▷It's not far.
　不遠。

▷It's pretty close.
　很近。

▷It's far away from here.
　離這裡很遠。

實·用·會·話 1

A : Excuse me, sir, but could you please tell
　　me how to get to the police station?

B : Well, it's a long way from here. You see
　　here you go ahead to the cross road,
　　then turn right. After 10 minutes' walk,
　　you'll see a hospital. The police station
　　is just opposite it.

A : Oh, so long a way!

B : Yes, but you can take No. 11 bus. It will

take you right there. The bus stop is just over there.

A：Very good! Thank you.

B：You're welcome.

A：對不起，先生，請問到警察局怎麼走？

B：噢，警察局離這兒很遠哪。看，你一直走，走到那個十字路口，然後向右轉，再走十分鐘，你會看到一家醫院，警察局就在那家醫院對面。

A：噢，好遠啊！

B：是的，不過你可以搭乘11號公共汽車，它會把你載到那裏。公共汽車站就在那邊。

A：太好了，謝謝。

B：不客氣。

深入分析

1. 英語中「問路」時通常要用 "Excuse me, ..." 開頭，以示禮貌，有「請問、打擾、麻煩您」的意思，也可以是請對方「借過」時使用，例如：

☑Excuse me, may I ask you a question?
  抱歉，我能問你一個問題嗎？

☑Excuse me, would you pass me the salt?

抱歉，能遞鹽給我嗎？

2. Could you please do …? 「您能……嗎？」

用來表達客氣的請求，例如：

☑Could you please pass me the salt?

請把鹽遞給我好嗎？

☑Could you please move over a little?

請挪開一些好嗎？

3. go ahead 意思是「一直走」，例如：

☑Go ahead till you get to the second crossing.

一直走到第二個十字路口。

實·用·會·話 2

A：Sorry to trouble you, sir, but I think I'm lost here.

Could you please tell me how I can arrive at Red Star Cinema?

B：Oh, I'm very sorry, but I'm a stranger here, too.

A：Thank you just the same.

B：Perhaps you can go ahead to ask that group of people. They seem to be the local ones.

A：Well, let me try. Thank you again.

B：You are welcome.

A：對不起，打擾你了，先生，我想我可能迷路了。請問到紅星影院怎麼走？

B：非常抱歉，我也是第一次來這兒。

A：還是得謝謝你。

B：你也許可以問問那一群人，他們好像是本地人。

A：嗯，讓我試試吧。再次謝謝你。

B：不客氣。

深入分析

1. Thank you just the same.

   這是在說話人不需要別人幫忙時所說的話。意思是「還是得謝謝你」。

2. seem to be 「看起來好像。」

   這是一種猜測的陳述句，例如：

   ☑She seems to be a nurse.

   她看起來像個護士。

   ☑It seems to be worse.

   好像事情不妙呀！

3. the local ones 的 ones 是指那一群人(people)。

實·用·會·話 3

A : Pardon me. Can you tell me where the B. H. Supermarket is?

B : Got me, pal. I'm a stranger here myself.

A : Well, thank you anyway.

C : Can I help you?

A : Yes. I'm trying to locate the B. H. Supermarket. I've been told it is somewhere near here, but I've been walking for quiet a while now and can't seem to find it.

C : Oh, it's right near here.

Just walk across the street and go around the corner on Green Road.

Walk one block east, take a right at 20th, then walk about half a block.

It's right in the middle of the block.

A : Would you mind drawing me a little map on this piece of paper?

C : Yes, it is easier to follow a map.

A : Is there any landmark there?

C : Oh, yes. You'll see a big apple poster.
You can't miss it.

A : Thanks a lot.

C : You are welcome.

A : 勞駕，請你告訴我B.H.超級市場在什麼地方
好嗎？

B : 你把我考倒了，朋友。我對這裏不熟悉。

A : 儘管如此，還是得謝謝你。

C : 我能幫你什麼忙嗎？

A : 是的。我正在找B.H.超級市場。有人告訴我
它就在這附近。可是我已經找了好一會兒
了，好像找不到。

C : 哦，就在這附近。
你只要橫過馬路，在格林大道拐角處繞過去
向東走一個街區。
在第二十街向右轉，然後走大約半個街區。
B.H.超級市場就在那一區的中間。

A : 請你在這張紙上幫我畫個路線圖好嗎？

C : 好的。有路線圖容易找些。

A：那個地方有路標嗎？

C：有的。你會看到一張大蘋果的海報。你不會
　　找不著的。

A：太感謝了。

C：不必客氣。

深入分析

> Would you mind...?「你介意……嗎？」
>
> 　通常用來向別人請求幫忙，是一種比較禮貌的說法，例如：
>
> ☑Would you mind closing the window?
> 　你介意把窗戶關上嗎？
>
> ☑ "Would you mind doing me a favor?"
> 　「你介意幫我個忙嗎？」
> 　"No."
> 　「不介意。」

實·用·會·話 4

A：Excuse me. Could you please tell me
　how to get to the station?

B：Turn left at the first light. You can't miss
　it.

A : Will it take me long to get there?

B : No. It's not far away.

A : Thank you.

B : Don't mention it.

A：對不起，請問到火車站怎麼走？

B：在第一個交通燈向左轉。你不會找不著的。

A：要花很久的時間到那裡嗎？

B：不遠。

A：謝謝你。

B：不客氣。

深入分析

　　到那裡會花我很多時間嗎？「Will it take me long to get there?」

　　是 It takes somebody some time to do something（某人花費多少時間做某事）的將來疑問句形式，例如：

☑It will take me a month to finish this job.

　　做完這工作，我要花一個月的時間。

☑It took me two hours to get there.

　　我花了二個小時的時間到達那裡。

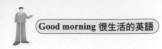

　　若是表示「我花了……(時間)完成某
事」，動詞則不用 take，而是用 spend 表
示，例如：

☑ I spend two hours to finish it.

　　我花了 2 個小時完成那件事。

打電話

• 去電 •

⮞Hello. May I speak to ...?
你好。請找……接電話好嗎？

⮞Hello. May I speak to..., please?
哈囉。我能和…說話嗎？

⮞Could I talk to... or...?
我可以找…或是…說話嗎？

⮞Hello. Is ...there?
你好。……在嗎？

⮞Hello. Is that ...?
你好。你是……嗎？

⮞Is Tom in, please?
請問湯姆在家嗎？

⮞Is... in today?
…今天在嗎？

⮞Extension 747, please.
請轉分機 747。

⮞Extension one hundred, please.
請轉分機 100。

➪I want to speak to ...
　我想和……通話。

➪May I speak to ...?
　我可以和……通話嗎？

➪This is Luke calling for....
　我是路克，打電話來要找…。

➪Is... in yet?
　……回來了嗎？

➪Is... off the line?
　……講完電話了嗎？

➪Is... in the office now?
　……現在在辦公室裡嗎？

➪Is this...?
　您是……嗎？

➪Do you know when he will be back?
　你知道他什麼時候會回來？

➪May I leave a message?
　我可以留言嗎？

➪I will call back later.
　我待會再撥。

➪I will try again later.
我晚一點再試。

➪When should I call back?
我什麼時候再打來好呢？

➪Would you ask him to call Betty at 8647-3663?
你能請他打電話到 8647-3663 給貝蒂嗎？

➪Would you tell him Jack returned his call?
請你告訴他傑克回過電話。

➪Tell him to give me a call as soon as possible.
告訴他盡快回我電話。

➪Do you know where I can reach him?
你知道我在哪裡可以聯絡上他嗎？

● 接電話 ●

➪This is Dr. Ford.
我就是福特教授。

➪This is he/she.
我就是本人。

➪Mark here.
我是馬克。

⮕Speaking.
請説。

⮕This is Bob speaking.
我是鮑伯。

⮕What is the name of the person you are calling?
你要通話的人是什麼名字？

⮕What is the number you are calling?
你打幾號？

⮕I can't talk to you now.
我現在不能講（電話）。

⮕Let me get back to you in a few minutes.
我幾分鐘後回你電話。

⮕Would you mind calling back later?
你介不介意待會再打電話來？

⮕May I ask who is calling?
請問您是哪位？

⮕Who is speaking, please?
請問你是哪一位？

⮕Who is this?
您是哪位？

⇨Hold on.
請等一下。

⇨Wait a minute, please.
請稍等。

⇨Just a minute, please.
請等一下。

⇨Would you please wait a moment?
能請你等一下嗎？

⇨Hold the line, please.
請稍等。

⇨Can you hold?
您要等嗎？

⇨Let me see for you.
我幫你看看。

⇨Let me see if she is in.
讓我確認她在不在。

⇨Let me see if he is available.
我看看他現在有沒有空。

⇨I will find out if he is in the office.
我會確認他是不是在辦公室。

➪He is not in yet.
　他現在還不在。

➪He is out to lunch.
　他出去用午餐了。

➪He is off today.
　他今天休假。

➪He is in a meeting now.
　他現在正在開會中。

➪He is in the middle of something.
　他正在忙。

➪He is busy with another line.
　他現在正在忙線中。

➪He is still on the phone.
　他還在講電話。

➪He won't be free until eleven thirty.
　他十一點卅分前不會有空。

➪The line is busy.
　電話占線中。

➪The line is engaged.
　電話占線中。

⇨Could you leave a message?
你需要留言嗎？

⇨Could I take a message?
我能幫你留言嗎？

⇨May I tell him who is calling?
需要我告訴他是誰來電嗎？

⇨I will have him return your call.
我會請他回你電話。

⇨I will call him for you.
我會幫你打電話給他。

⇨I will get him.
我去叫他（來聽電話）。

⇨I will put you through to him immediately.
我立刻幫您轉給他。

⇨I will put your call through.
我替您轉電話。

⇨Thank you for waiting.
謝謝你等這麼久。

⇨Sorry to have kept you waiting.
抱歉讓你久等了。

實·用·會·話 1

A：Hello!

B：Is John there?

A：Speaking. Who is calling?

B：It's Tom calling. It's a long distance call from Macao!
Can't you hear me? I say I'm now in Macao!

A：Oh! What are you doing there?

B：It's a long story, but I'll make it short to you. I've lost all my money to the casino and can't get back to Hong Kong.

A：You fool! Why should you go to such places?

B：Give me no lessons now, please. Just come to me right now. I'll meet you at the hydrofoils. Be quick!

A：喂！

B：約翰在嗎？

A：我就是。誰呀？

B：我是湯姆，從澳門打長途電話給你。聽到了

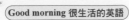

嗎？我說我現在在澳門呀！

A：噢，你到澳門做什麼？

B：說來話長了，我長話短說吧。我在賭場輸光了錢，不能返回香港啦。

A：蠢材！到那種地方去幹嘛？

B：現在不要教訓我了。馬上來幫幫我吧。我在水翼船碼頭等你。快些！

1. Give me no lessons.「不要再教訓我了。」

此句是從 Give somebody a lesson. 引申而來，意思是「教訓某人一頓」，例如：

☑ I'll let him know who I am by giving him a lesson.

我要教訓他一頓，讓他知道我是誰。

2. I'll make it short to you.「我長話短說吧。」

這裏的 it 代表 the long story，short 作 make 的受詞補語。

實·用·會·話 2

A：Hello, is Jenny in?

B：No, I'm afraid she's out at the moment.

Who is speaking, please?

A：Sophia, her friend from Taiwan. May I leave a message?

B：Certainly. Just a moment, please. I need to get a pencil. OK. What is it please?

A：Would you please tell her to call back this afternoon? I'll be expecting her call then.

B：What's your number please?

A：86473663. Thank you very much.

B：You are welcome.

A：喂，珍妮在嗎？

B：不，她現在還沒回來。請問你是哪一位？

A：我是蘇菲亞，她的台灣朋友。可以留言嗎？

B：當然可以。請稍等。我需要支鉛筆。好啦，請問留什麼話？

A：請你告訴她今天下午給我回個電話好嗎？到時我等著。

B：請問你的號碼是多少？

A：86473663。非常感謝。

B：不必客氣。

Would you please...? 「能請你…嗎？」

這是一個很有用的句型，用來表示客氣的請求，例如：

☑Would you please help me with my luggage?
請你幫我拿一下我的行李好嗎？

☑Would you please move over a little?
請你向一邊靠靠好嗎？

實·用·會·話 3

A：Hello. May I speak to Ailing, please?

B：Oh, just a minute please. Ailing, it'sfor you.

C：Hello, this is Ailing speaking. Who is it, please?

A：This is David speaking.

There is a very good film on in the local cinema.

Would you like to go with me tonight?

C：What is the name of the film?

A：The Bridges of Madison County.

打電話

C：Ah, it's really a wonderful film. I'd love to go.

A：I'll come and pick you up at six o'clock. The movie starts at six thirty.

C：All right. See you then.

A：喂，請讓愛玲聽電話。

B：哦，請稍等。愛玲，你的電話。

C：喂，我是愛玲，請問是哪位？

A：我是大衛。

本地電影院正在上映一部非常好的電影。

你今晚想跟我去嗎？

C：電影的名字是什麼？

A：《麥迪遜大橋》。

C：啊，真的是一部好電影，我想去。

A：六點鐘我來接你。電影六點半開始。

C：好吧。到時見。

 深入分析

1.There is... on 這裏的 on 是副詞，表示「（電影）放映、（戲劇）上演、（展覽）展出、（音樂）播放等」，例如：

☑There is an exhibition of Chinese oil paintings on at the Art Gallery.

在藝術博物館有個中國油畫展覽正在展出。

☑I looked over the TV Guide to see if there was any interesting program on.

我瀏覽《電視導報》，看看有沒有有趣的節目放映。

2.I'd love to 用來表達「願意、樂意去做某事」，通常是回覆對方的邀約。若是不答應，則可以說：I'd love to... but I...表示「我很想去，但是我…因為…，所以不能去」加以拒絕，例如：

☑ "Would you like to go for an outing with me?"

「你想和我一起去郊遊嗎？」

"I'd love to."

「我很樂意（去）。」

"I'd love to, but I have other planes."

「我很想去，但是我有其他計畫了。」

實·用·會·話 4

A：Sales Section.

B：Is Mr. Brown in?

A：Speaking.

B：Oh, hello, Mr. Brown. This is Peter speaking. How are you?

A：Just fine, thanks. What can I do for you?

B：Well, I was wondering if I could drop in for a few minutes today.

A：We're a little busy today. Can you come right away?

B：I think I can make it in ten minutes or so.

A：Fine. I'll be expecting you.

B：Thanks, see you in a few minutes.

A：這是營業部。

B：布朗先生在嗎？

A：我就是。

B：哦，布朗先生，你好。我是彼得，你好嗎？

A：還好，謝謝。有何指教？

B：嗯，我在想今天是否能打擾你一會兒。

A：我們今天有點忙。你能馬上來嗎？

B：我想我十分鐘左右就可以到你那裏。

A：好的。我等你。

B：多謝了。等會兒見。

深入分析

1. I was wondering if I could drop in for a few minutes. 「我在想不知能否拜託你，耽誤你幾分鐘的時間。」

   (1) I was wondering if … 是 I wonder if … 更為禮貌的形式，意思是「不知道（能否）……」，例如：

☑ I was wondering if you could spare me a few minutes.

不知道我能否耽擱你幾分鐘時間？

   (2) drop in 為動詞+副詞結構的片語動詞，意思是「拜訪」，例如：

☑ I was about to leave home when several friends dropped in.

我正要離家時，有幾位朋友來訪。

2. I can make it. 「我能做到／成功」。

這裏的 it 並沒有什麼實際意義，只是單純的受詞，例如：

☑ They made it at last.

他們終於成功了。

☑ Can you make it?

你做得到/趕得及嗎？

實·用·會·話 5

A：Hello.

B：Hello. May I speak to Mary, please?

A：Speaking.

B：Hi, Mary. This is Tom Johnson.

A：Oh, hi, Tom. How have you been?

B：Just fine. Listen, Mary, I called to ask if you are busy tomorrow evening.

A：Let me see. No, I don't think I've got anything planned.

B：Well, I thought we might have dinner together and go to the movies.

A：Oh, that sounds like fun.

B：I'll pick you up at 6:00 then.

A：Thanks! I'll see you tomorrow. Bye, Tom.

B：Bye, Mary.

A：喂。

B：喂。請找瑪麗聽電話。

A：我就是。

B：嗨，瑪麗。我是湯姆‧強生。

A：噢，嗨，湯姆。近來好嗎？

B：很好。瑪麗，我打電話是要問明天晚上你有沒有空。

A：我想想，我想我還沒有計劃要做什麼。有事嗎？

B：噢，我想我們可以共進晚餐，然後一起去看電影。

A：哦，聽起來很有趣。

B：那麼我六點來接你。

A：謝謝，明天見。再見，湯姆。

B：再見，瑪麗。

實‧用‧會‧話 6

A：Hello.

B：Hello. May I speak to Kenny, please?

A：I'm sorry. He's not in right now. Who's calling, please?

B：This is Jim, his former classmate.

A：Hi, Jim. Can I take a message?

B：Yes. Please ask him to call me at

86473663.

A：Was that 86473663?

B：Yes.

A：OK. I'll give him the message. Goodbye, Jim.

B：Thank you. Goodbye.

A：喂。

B：喂。請找肯尼聽電話。

A：對不起，他現在不在。請問你是哪一位？

B：我是吉姆，他以前的同學。

A：嗨，吉姆。要不要我傳話？

B：好。請叫他打 86473663 找我。

A：是 86473663 嗎？

B：對。

A：好的。我會轉告他。再見。

B：謝謝。再見。

實·用·會·話 7

A：Hello. May I speak to Jenny, please?

B：Oh, just a minute please. Jenny, it's for you.

(Later)

C：Hello, this is Jenny speaking. Who is it, please?

A：This is Tom speaking. Would you like to see a movie with me tonight?

C：What is the name of the film?

A：The Lord of The Ring.

C：Ah, it's really a wonderful film. I'd love to go.

A：喂。請找珍妮聽電話。

B：噢，請等一下。珍妮，找你的。

（稍後）

C：喂，我是珍妮。請問你是哪一位？

A：我是湯姆。本地電影院有部非常好的電影。今天晚上你想和我一起去嗎？

C：什麼電影啊？

A：《魔戒首部曲》。

C：啊，確實是一部好電影。我去。

深入分析

1.Would you like (to) ...?「你想……嗎?」
是一句非常口語的邀約或詢問句型,例如:
☑ Would you like a cup of tea?

你想來杯茶嗎?
☑ Would you like to join us?

你想加入我們嗎?
2.I'll come and pick you up at six o'clock.

「我六點鐘來接你。」
pick up 為動詞+副詞結構片語動詞,意思
是「接(某人)」,例如:
☑ Granny comes to school to pick up Tom
every day.

奶奶每天來學校接湯姆。

實·用·會·話 8

A:Hello.

B:Hello. May I speak to Mark, please?

A:Sure, just a minute. Mark, you're wan-
ted on the phone.

C:Hello, this is Mark speaking.

B:Hi! This is Kent. How come you didn't

come in today?

C : Oh, we had a farewell party for David last night.

As a matter of fact I woke up with a terrible hangover.

B : That's too bad. You'll have to be more careful next time.

C : Anything new at the office?

B : No, nothing special. Oh, yes, you know Bill, the guy with the moustache. His wife had a baby girl last nigh. He said his wife and daughter are doing fine.

C : That's wonderful! We've got to celebrate!

B : Yes, we have to. Do you think you can make it tomorrow?

C : Sure. I ought to get ready for some more drinks by then. Thank you for calling.

B : You're welcome. Bye.

A：喂。

B：喂。請找馬克聽電話。

A：好啊，等一下。馬克，你的電話。

C：喂，我是馬克。

B：嗨！我是肯特。你今天怎麼沒來上班？

C：噢，昨晚我們為大衛舉行歡送會。事實上，我醒來後發現有嚴重的宿醉。

B：真糟糕。下次你該小心點兒。

C：今天辦公室有什麼新鮮事嗎？

B：沒什麼別的。噢，對了，你知道那個留鬍子的比爾。他太太昨晚生了個女孩，他說他太太和女兒目前都很平安。

C：太棒了！我們一定得慶祝一下！

B：是該慶祝一下。你想你明天可以嗎？

C：當然可以。我應該要有到時候多喝一點的準備。謝謝你打電話來。

B：不客氣。再見。

深入分析

1. How come you didn't come yesterday?「為什麼你昨天沒來？」

    How come ...?是個很口語化的說法，意思是詢問原因，例如：

☑How come you didn't appear at the dancing party?

你怎麼沒有去參加舞會呢？

2. make it 這個片語具有寬泛的意義，如「能做到、成功、完成等」，要視所要表達的實際狀況來決定其意思，例如：

☑I can't make it in two months.

我無法在兩個月的時間內完成。

☑Stand up! You can make it!

站起來！你能做到的！

實·用·會·話 9

A：Hello.

B：Hello. This is Mrs. Lee in Apt. 212. May I speak with the manager, please?

A：This is he.

B：I've a problem in my apartment. The faucets on my kitchen sink are stuck. I can't turn them off.

A：I'm getting ready to go home now. That doesn't seem like a big problem. Could you wait until tomorrow?

B：What do you mean it's not a big problem? What about the flood in my kitchen?

A：OK. I'll be up there right away.

A：喂。

B：喂。我是 212 號公寓的李太太。我想找經理
聽電話。

A：我就是。有什麼需要我服務的嗎？

B：我的公寓出了點問題。我廚房水槽的水龍頭
卡住了。我沒有辦法把水關掉。

A：我現在已經準備好要回家了。看起來那不是
什麼大問題。你能等到明天嗎？

B：你說不是什麼大問題是什麼意思？那我廚房
淹水怎麼辦？

A：好吧，我馬上就到。

深入分析

turn off/on 表示電器「關閉打開電源」的
意思，若是門窗的關閉/打開，則要用 close/
open 表示，例如：

☑turn off
- the TV 關電視
- the radio 關收音機
- the light 關燈

☑close
- the door 關門
- the window 關窗

實·用·會·話 10

A : Good morning. Evans Company. May I help you?

B : Could I speak to Mr. Smith, please?

A : I'll see if he is available. Who shall I say is calling, please?

B : Bill Gorden.

A : Hold the line, please.

（Later）

A : Mr. Smith is in a meeting with the Managing Director at the moment, I'm afraid. What can I help you?

B : Well, I want to discuss with him the new contract we signed last week.

A : I don't think the meeting will go on much longer.

Shall I ask him to call you when he is free?

B: Yes, that could be easiest.

A: Could I have your name again, please?

B: It's Bill Gorden.

A: And the number?

B: 86473663.

A: Right. You'll be hearing from Mr. Smith later in the morning then, Mr. Gorden.

B: Thank you for your help. Goodbye.

A: You are welcome. Goodbye.

A: 早安，這是埃文思公司，我能替你效勞嗎？

B: 我能找史密斯先生嗎？

A: 我去看看他是否有空。請問你是哪位？

B: 我是比爾·戈登。

A: 請稍候！

（稍後）

A: 史密斯先生和總經理正在開會。我能幫忙嗎？

B: 噢，我想和他討論上週簽定的合約。

A: 我想會議不會開得太久。他有空時再讓他回

電話給你好嗎？

B：好，那太好了。

A：請再告訴我您的大名好嗎？

B：我叫比爾‧戈登。

A：您的電話號碼是多少？

B：8647366。

A：好的，戈登先生，史密斯先生會在今天上午給您回話的。

B：謝謝你幫忙，再見。

A：不客氣，再見。

1. When is a person not a person?

   什麼時候人不是人？

2. What's the different between fly and mosquito?

   蒼蠅和蚊子有什麼不同？

1. When he is a little cross.

   當他有點惱怒時。

   原來如此

   cross 除了當「發怒」解釋之外，也有「路口」的意思。

2. A fly can fly, but a mosquito can't mosquito.

   蒼蠅可以飛，但是蚊子不能蚊子。

   原來如此

   fly可以同時是名詞「蒼蠅」和動詞「飛」的意思，所以蒼蠅可以飛（fly），但是mosquito只有名詞蚊子的意思，因此不能用mosquito當動詞。

談論天氣

▷It's nice today, isn't it?
今天天氣不錯呀，不是嗎？

▷It's a bit cloudy, isn't it?
今天是多雲的，不是嗎？

▷Lovely weather, isn't it?
天氣很好，不是嗎？

▷It's a perfect day for shopping.
今天適合去購物。

▷What a lovely day.
天氣真好。

▷The weather is terrible.
天氣糟透了！

▷It's an awful day.
真是糟糕的一天。

▷It's very hot today.
今天非常熱！

▷It's a nice day.
天氣真好。

▷It's warm.
天氣暖和。

⇨It's humid.
天氣潮濕。

⇨It's dry.
天氣乾燥。

⇨It's foggy.
起霧了。

⇨It's snowing.
下雪了。

⇨It's raining now.
現正在下雨。

⇨It's cold.
天氣很冷。

⇨It's chilly.
冷颼颼的。

⇨It's freezing today.
今天冷死了。

⇨It's bitterly cold today.
今天特別冷。

⇨It's snowing heavily.
雪下得很大。

➪It's windy this afternoon.
下午風很大。

➪It's rather windy today.
今天風真大。

➪It'll clear up tomorrow.
明天會晴天。

➪It'll clear up soon.
很快就會放晴。

➪It's a little cloudy.
天氣有一點多雲。

➪It's getting cloudy.
雲越來越多了。

➪It'll be a wet day, I'm afraid.
恐怕會下雨。

➪Is it going to rain today?
今天會下雨嗎？

➪It's going to rain soon.
很快就會下雨。

➪It's only a shower.
只是小雨。

⇨It's getting warmer day by day.
越來越暖和了。

⇨Spring is my favorite season.
春天是我最喜歡的季節。

⇨It's already spring.
已經春天了。

⇨Spring is almost over.
春天快結束了。

⇨How is the weather today?
今天天氣如何？

⇨What will the weather be like tomorrow?
明天天氣會怎麼樣？

⇨What does the weather forecast say?
天氣預報怎麼說？

⇨What's the weather forecast for tomorrow?
氣象預報說明天天氣如何？

⇨What's the temperature today?
今天溫度是多少？

⇨The temperature has climbed to 36 ℃.
溫度已經上升到了攝氏36度。

實·用·會·話 1

A：What a lovely day!

B：Yes, isn't it?

A：Do you think it will also be the same tomorrow?

B：I hope so. But the weather is changeable in spring here. So when you go out, you'd better take an umbrella with you.

A：天氣多好呀！

B：可不是嗎？

A：你是否認為明天天氣也一樣好呢？

B：希望是這樣吧，但在這裏春季的天氣是多變的，所以當你外出時最好帶上雨傘。

實·用·會·話 2

A：A beautiful day, isn't it?

B：Yes. Nice and sunny for a change.

A：It's so great to see sunshine again after those rainy days.

B：I prefer sunny days to rainy days.

A：多好的天氣，對嗎？

B：是呀，總算風和日暖了。

A：久雨之後再見到陽光，真是太好了。

B：我喜歡和煦的日子，不太喜歡下雨的日
　子。

 深入分析

> prefer A to B 意思是「比起 B 來，更喜歡
> A」，例如：
> ☑ I prefer tea to coffee.
> 　茶和咖啡，我更喜歡前者。
> 　另外，若是動作相比而後作出選擇，則用
> prefer to do than do 句型，例如：
> ☑ I prefer to stay at home than go to watch the
> film.
> 　我寧願待在家裏也不願去看電影。

實·用·會·話 3

A：I wonder what the weather will be like
　tomorrow.

B：I haven't heard the weather report on
　the radio. But I expect it will be warm,
　too.

A：I think so. It seems days are getting longer and longer.

B：Yes. Summer is around the corner.

A：Many people, especially the young people, are looking forward to its coming.

B：Right. It is a season of sports.

A：不知道明天的天氣會怎麼樣。

B：我沒有聽到收音機播的天氣預報，但我希望天氣會變溫暖。

A：我也這樣想。看起來白天的時間變得越來越長了。

B：是的。夏天快要到了。

A：我想很多人，特別是年輕人都盼望夏天的來臨。

B：對的，那是運動的季節。

 深入分析

Summer is around the corner.「夏天就快來了。」

around the corner 字面意思是「在角落」，也就是「在附近、將來臨」的意思，例如：

☑ "Where is he?"

「他在哪兒？」

"He is just around the corner."

「他就在附近。」

☑ The Spring Festival is around the corner.

春節就要到了。

實·用·會·話 4

A : I'm afraid we'll have a very hot summer this year. I don't know where to go for my summer vacation.

B : Why don't you go to the countryside? The weather will be cooler there.

A : Good idea! Do you often spend summer holidays in the mountains?

B : Yes. I enjoy cooler weather and I can visit my grandparents.

A : 恐怕我們今年會有一個酷熱的夏季。我不知道去哪裡過暑假。

B : 為什麼不到鄉下去呢？那裏的天氣較涼快。

A : 好主意！你經常在山上度暑假嗎？

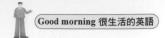

B：是的，我可以享受涼快的夏天，而且還能探望我的祖父母。

實·用·會·話 5

A：嗨！比爾，今天好嗎？

B：我很好，謝謝。今天天氣真好！

A：做事的好日子。

B：的確如此。

A：回頭見。

B：好的，保羅。回頭見。

A：Hello, Bill. How are you today?

B：Fine, thanks. Beautiful day!

A：Good for business.

B：Sure is.

A：See you later.

B：O.K. Paul. See you later.

Unit 9

日期與時間

・問句・ ●

➪What is today's date?
今天幾號？

➪What date is it today?
今天幾號？

➪What's the date today?
今天幾號？

➪What day is it?
今天星期幾？

➪What time is it now?
現在幾點了？

➪What's the time?
幾點了？

➪How goes the time?
幾點了？

➪Do you have the time?
你知道現在幾點？

➪Have you got the time?
你知道幾點了嗎？

➪What time do you have? My watch seems to be slow.

你知道幾點了嗎？我的錶好像慢了。

➪What time is it by your watch? Mine seems to be fast.

你的錶幾點了？我的錶好像快了。

➪Could you tell me the time?
你能告訴我幾點了嗎？

➪May I ask the time?
請問現在幾點？

➪Is your watch right?
你的錶準嗎？

➪Does your watch keep good time?
你的錶時間準確嗎？

➪Isn't your watch a bit fast?
你的錶是不是有點快？

•回答•••••••••••••••••••••••••••

➪It's May first.
今天五月一日。

➪It's the fifteenth of January.
  今天一月十五日。

➪It's Sunday.
  今天星期天。

➪It's half past nine.
  九點半。

➪It's fifteen after three.
  三點十五分。

➪It's seven o'clock sharp.
  七點整。

➪It's exactly ten o'clock. I just heard the signal.
  十點整。我剛聽到鐘響。

➪It's a quarter to eleven.
  差十五分就十一點（十點四十五分）。

➪It's ten after two.
  現在兩點十分。

➪It's eight five.
  八點過五分。

➪It's eight forty-five.

八點四十五分。

⇨It's midday (noon).
十二點。

⇨It's almost noon.
快要中午了。

⇨It's mid-night.
午夜十二點。

⇨It's one forty p.m.
下午一點四十分。

⇨It's eleven forty a.m.
上午十一點四十分。

⇨It's sixteen hundred hours Taipei Time.
台北時間十六點。

⇨It's twenty-one hundred hours GMT.
格林威治時間二十一點。

⇨My watch says it's six o'clock.
我的手表現在是六點。

⇨It keeps good time.
這錶走得很準。

➩It gains thirty seconds a day.
它每天快三十秒。

➩It loses about two minutes a day.
它每天慢兩分鐘。

➩It's ten minutes slow.
慢 10 分鐘。

➩It's ten minutes fast.
快 10 分鐘。

➩It loses a bit.
它有點慢。

●時間表示● ● ● ● ● ● ● ● ● ● ● ● ● ● ● ● ● ● ●

➩Time is up.
時間到了。

➩No more time.
沒時間了。

➩Time to go home.
回家的時間到了。

➩Time to say good-bye.
該說再見了。

▷Time for bed.
上床的時間到了。

▷It's about time to leave.
該離開的時間到了。

▷Now is the time to fight back.
該是反擊的時候了。

▷It's about time for my departure.
我該離境的時間到了。

▷I have plenty of time.
我的時間還很多。

▷I don't have any time.
我沒有任何時間。

▷I have no time for novels.
我沒有空閒看小說。

▷I have no time.
我沒空。

▷Got a minute?
有空嗎？

▷You are wasting my time.
你在浪費我的時間。

▷The plane is timed to arrive at five.
飛機定於五點抵達。

▷It's on time.
準時。

▷It's in time.
即時。

▷It's late.
遲到了。

▷It's early.
還很早。

▷How much time can you get?
你有多少時間？

▷How much time is left?
還剩多少時間？

▷How much time is spent in each activity?
每個活動花多少時間？

▷How many times did you do?
你做過幾次了？

實·用·會·話 1

A：What time is it now?

B：Oh, my watch has stopped. I must have forgotten to wind it last night. Ask Mary.

A：Mary, have you got the time?

C：Yes, it's nine twenty.

B：Is your watch right?

C：I think so. I set it by the radio this morning.

A：How time flies! Let's call it a day.

B：Yes, let's go back to our dorm.

A：現在幾點了？

B：哦，我的錶停了。昨天晚上我一定忘了給錶上發條。問問瑪麗吧。

A：瑪麗，你知道時間嗎？

C：知道，九點廿分了。

B：你的錶準嗎？

C：我想是的。今天早上我跟著收音機對時了一下。

A：時間過得真快呀！今天就到這裏吧。

B：好，我們回宿舍吧。

深入分析

　　Let's call it a day. 意思是「我們今天就到這裏為止吧」是「停止、結束目前手頭上的事」之意，例如；

☑ We worked successively for eight hours and then called it a day to go home.

　　我們連續工作了八小時，然後就回家了。

實·用·會·話 2

A：What's the time, David?

B：My watch says seven o'clock.

A：Does your watch keep good time?

B：Yes, it keeps very good time. It's one of those new digital watches which are very reliable. One small battery keeps it running accurately for at least a year.

A：That's very convenient. I hope I have one like yours.

B：But yours is nice, too.

A：It was, but it gains six minutes a day recently. I've got to have it repaired.

A：大衛，幾點了？

B：我的手錶是七點鐘。

A：你的手錶很準嗎？

B：是的，很準。這是幾種不錯的新型電子錶之一。一個小號電池可以用上至少一年。

A：那到是挺方便的。我希望有你那樣的錶。

B：你的錶也不錯呀。

A：以前還可以。但最近一天快六分鐘。我得去修理修理。

 深入分析

1. keep good time 意思是「錶的時間很準」。

2. gains six minutes a day. 意思是「每天快六分鐘」，例如：

☑My watch gains a little everyday.

我的錶每天總是快一點兒。

實·用·會·話 3

(A foreign guest is asking David the time.)

A：Excuse me, could you tell me the time?

B：Yes, it's five to eight by my watch.

A: What's the time you use here?

B: We are on Taipei Time. It's the standard time for the whole country.

A: What's the difference between your time and GMT?

B: There's a difference of eight hours. When it is nine o'clock in the morning in London, it's five o'clock in the afternoon of the same day here.

A: Oh, I see. When people in my country have just begun the day's work, people here are ready to get off work.

B: That's right.

（一外國人賓客正在問大衛時間）

A：對不起，你能告訴我現在的時間嗎？

B：好的，我的錶是還有五分鐘八點。

A：你們這裏採用什麼時間？

B：我們採用台北時間，這是全國的標準時間。

A：台北時間和格林威治時間有什麼區別？

B：八小時之差。當倫敦是早上九點鐘的時候，這裏是同一天的下午五點。

A：哦，明白了。當我們國家的人們剛剛開始一
天的工作的時候，這裏的人們正準備下班。

B：對。

 深入分析

1. GMT 是 Greenwich Mean Time（格林威
   治時間）的縮寫形式。

2. Taipei Time 台北時間

3. get off work 意思是「下班」，例如：
   ☑We usually get off at 5 pm.
   我們通常下午五點下班。

實·用·會·話 4

A：Excuse me, do you have the time?

B：Sorry, I don't have my watch with me.

A：Thanks anyway.

A：對不起，請問幾點了？

B：抱歉，我沒有帶錶。

A：還是謝謝你。

實·用·會·話 5

A：What time does your train leave?

B：At 12:30 pm.

A：Then we still have plenty of time.

A：你乘坐的火車幾點鐘開？

B：中午十二點半。

A：那麼我們還有很多時間。

實·用·會·話 6

A：What time do you usually get up?

B：At half past six, except on Saturdays and Sundays when I get up an hour later.

A：And when do you have your meals?

B：I have breakfast at seven, lunch at twelve, and dinner at six in the evening.

A：你通常幾點鐘起床？

B：六點半，但星期六、星期天晚起一小時。

A：那麼，幾點鐘吃飯？

B：早餐七點，午餐十二點，晚餐則是六點。

1. Why is tennis so noisy?

   打網球為什麼很吵?

2. If a cabbage and a carrot raced, which one would win?

   如果包心菜和胡蘿蔔賽跑，誰會贏?

3. How many feet are there in a yard?

   一碼有多少英尺?

1. Each player raises a racket.

   因為每個運動員都拿著球拍。

   原來如此

   因為 racket 除了是「球拍」，也是「吵鬧」的意思。

2. The cabbage, because it's always ahead.

   包心菜，因為它總是領先在前。

   原來如此

   因為 cabbage 有偷竊布料的意思。

3. It depends on how many people stand in the yard.

   這要看院子裏站了多少人。

   原來如此

   因為 feet 除了是「英尺」之外，也是「腳」的意思。

關心健康

• 表示身體健康 • • • • • • • • • • • • • • • • • • •

⇨I can't eat.
我吃不下。

⇨I can't sleep.
我睡不著。

⇨I can't stop coughing.
我咳嗽不止。

⇨I can't stop sneezing.
我不停地打噴嚏。

⇨I can't stop shivering.
我不停地打顫。

⇨I don't feel well.
我覺得不舒服。

⇨I am not feeling well.
我覺得不舒服。

⇨I have a cold.
我感冒了。

⇨I have a bad cold.
我得了重感冒。

▷I have a fever.
　我發燒了。

▷I have a headache.
　我頭痛。

▷I have a ringing in my ears.
　我耳鳴。

▷I have a stuffy nose.
　我流鼻水。

▷I have a toothache.
　我牙痛。

▷I have a cavity.
　我蛀牙。

▷I have a sore throat.
　我喉嚨痛。

▷I have a canker sore.
　我嘴破。

▷I have a hiccup.
　我打嗝。

▷I have stiff shoulders.
　我肩膀痠痛。

➪I have a stomachache.
我胃痛。

➪I have diarrhea.
我拉肚子。

➪I have a chill.
我在打顫。

➪I feel dizzy.
我覺得頭暈。

➪I feel painful.
我覺得痛。

➪I feel tired.
我覺得很累。

➪I feel dull.
我覺得頭鈍鈍。

➪I feel sick.
我感覺不舒服。

➪I feel like throwing up.
我想要嘔吐。

➪I feel much better.
我覺得好多了。

➪I don't have any appetite.
　我沒有食慾。

➪I can't breathe well.
　我呼吸不順。

➪I am constipated.
　我便秘。

➪I am injured.
　我扭傷了。

➪I sprained my neck.
　我扭傷脖子。

➪I sprained my finger.
　我扭傷手指。

➪I sprained my ankle.
　我扭傷腳踝。

➪I broke my leg.
　我摔斷腿。

➪I ache all over.
　我渾身痠痛。

➪My head hurts.
　我頭痛。

➪My nose is running.
　我流鼻水。

➪My foot is killing me.
　我的腳痛死了。

➪My heart is pounding.
　我心跳得很厲害。

➪It hurts.
　好痛。

➪It's bleeding.
　流血了。

➪She passed out.
　她暈過去了。

➪I need to see a doctor.
　我需要看醫生。

➪I would like to see a doctor.
　我需要看醫生。

➪Could you call an ambulance?
　你可以叫救護車嗎？

•詢問對方• • • • • • • • • • • • • • • • •

➪You look terrible.
你臉色看起來糟透了！

➪You look pale.
你看起來臉色蒼白。

➪You don't look very well.
你的狀況看起來不太好。

➪Do you need any help?
你需要幫助嗎？

➪Do you need a doctor?
你需要看醫生嗎？

➪Do you want me to call an ambulance?
需要我叫救護車嗎？

➪What's wrong with you?
你有什麼問題嗎？

➪What are your symptoms?
你的症狀是什麼？

➪How are you today?
你今天怎麼樣？

⇨How do you feel now?
你現在覺得如何？

⇨What did you eat last night?
你昨晚吃了什麼？

⇨Let me check your blood pressure.
讓我量量你的血壓。

實·用·會·話 1

A：Hello, George. You look rather pale to-day. Are you Okay?

B：I am staying home from work.

A：What's wrong?

B：It's a bad cold.

A：I hope you'll get over it soon.

A：你好，喬治。你今天臉色很蒼白。你沒事吧？

B：我正休假在家。

A：怎麼不舒服？

B：重感冒。

A：希望你早日康復。

深入分析

1. look＋adj. 是個很有用的句型，意思是「看起來…」，如：

☑ You look smart today.

你今天看起來很帥。

☑ You look great.

你看起來神情氣爽。

2. Staying home from work 意思是「待在家裏不去上班」。

3. Get over it 意思是「康復」，非常適合用於安慰的情境。

實·用·會·話 2

A：Hi, Mary. How are you today?

B：I'm not feeling well today. As a matter of fact, I'm going to see the doctor in the school clinic.

A：What's the matter?

B：I've got a sore throat. It gives me so much pain that I can hardly eat.

A：Feel better soon.

A：你好，瑪麗。今天好嗎？

B：我今天感覺不好。實際上，我要去學校診所看醫生。

A：怎麼不舒服？

B：喉嚨痛。疼得我幾乎不能吃飯。

A：祝你早日康復。

實·用·會·話 3

A：How are you feeling today? Are you all right?

B：I'm O.K., except that I've got a bad cough.

A：Oh dear, I'm sorry to hear that. How did it happen?

B：I was caught in the rain yesterday and ran a fever during the night.
I took some aspirin, and when I woke up this morning, the fever was gone; but I started to cough.

A：You should get some cough syrup. If it gets worse, you should see your doctor.

B：Yes, I will. Thank you very much.

A：你今天感覺怎麼樣？還好吧？

B：還好，只是咳嗽不止。

A：哦，聽你這麼說，我很難過。怎麼搞的？

B：昨天我淋了雨，夜裏就發燒。

　　我吃了一些阿司匹林，早上醒來，燒退了，

　　但我開始咳嗽。

A：你應服用止咳糖漿。再不好的話，你就應該

　　去看醫生。

B：好，我會的。非常感謝。

深入分析

> be caught in the rain 意思是「被雨淋」，
> 例如：
>
> ☑He was caught in the rain and wet all over.
>
> 他被雨淋溼了，全身都濕透了。

實·用·會·話 4

A：How's your dad coming along after the operation on his eye?

B：He's recovered well. And he's now up and about again.

A：But he's staying home from work, isn't he?

B：Yes. The doctor told him not to move too much and to have plenty of rest. On top of that he should not do any reading for the time being.

A：That's perhaps the last piece of advice he would like to follow.

B：Absolutely. And that's why he's feeling a little upset lately.

A：I hope he'll take it easy and feel like himself soon.

B：It's very kind of you to say so. Dad will be glad to hear that you asked after him.

A：你爸爸眼部手術後恢復得怎樣？

B：恢復得很好。現在已經能起床四處走動了。

A：但他現在家休養，沒去上班，是吧？

B：是的。醫生告訴他要少活動，多休息。最重要的是目前不應該閱讀任何東西。

A：那恐怕是他最不願意聽從的忠告。

B：對極了。這就是為什麼他最近有點煩躁。

A：希望他放輕鬆點，一切都會轉好。

B：感謝你的關心。爸爸聽到了會非常高興的。

 深入分析

1. up and about 是副詞片語，意即「起來四處走動」，通常用來指病後恢復健康的人的活動狀況。

2. the last piece of advice 意思是「最不願聽的建議」。類似的句子如：

☑ He is the last man I want to see.
他是我最不願意見的人。

3. feel like himself 意思是「感覺自如」、「完全恢復」，例如：

☑ It was not long before he felt like himself again.
不久他就完全恢復了。

實·用·會·話 5

A：I haven't seen Bob lately. How is he?

B：As a matter of fact, he's laid up.

A：Oh, dear! What's up with him?

B：We don't know, but we're having the

doctor in tomorrow.

A：Let me know if there's anything I can do.

B：Thank you very much. I'll tell him you
inquired about him.

A：我最近都沒有見到鮑勃。他好嗎？

B：說實在的，他病倒了。

A：哦，天哪！他得了什麼病？

B：我們不知道，不過我們準備明天請醫生來。

A：如果有什麼我能幫忙的，請告訴我。

B：非常感謝。我會告訴他你問起過他。

 深入分析

　　As a matter of fact 意思是「事實上、實際
上」，如：

☑ As a matter of fact, he a very selfish person.

　　實際上，他是個很自私的人。

☑ "I suppose you haven't finished that report
yet？"

　　「我猜你還沒有完成那份報告？」

　　"I finished it yesterday, as a matter of fact."

　　「事實上我昨天就完成了。」

1. When are people like glasses?

   什麼時候人像眼鏡？

2. What beam is lighter than all the other beams?

   什麼樑最輕？

英語腦筋急轉彎 解答

1. When they make spectacles of themselves.

   當他們出洋相的時候。

   原來如此

   make a spectacle oneself 表示出洋相，spectacle
   又指「眼鏡」。

2. Light beam.

   光線。

   原來如此

   beam 除了「樑」之外，又表示「光線」之意。

160

談好惡

・問句・ • • • • • • • • • • • • • • • •

➱Do you have any hobbies?
你有什麼嗜好嗎？

➱What are you hobbies?
你的嗜好是什麼？

➱What are you interested in?
你對什麼有興趣？

➱What types of things do you want to try?
你想嘗試哪方面的事物？

➱What kind of books do you read?
你都看哪些書呢？

➱What kind of sports do you like?
喜歡什麼運動呢？

➱What sort of music do you like?
你喜歡什麼類型的音樂？

➱What kind of book do you like?
你喜歡什麼類型的書籍？

➱What's your favorite sports?
你最喜歡什麼運動？

What do you think about this movie?
你覺得這部電影怎麼樣？

What do you think of this book?
你覺得這本書怎麼樣？

Who's your favorite singer?
你最喜歡的歌手是誰？

What's your favorite TV program?
你喜歡哪個電視節目？

What do you usually do during weekends?
週末你通常都做些什麼事？

How many books do you read a month?
你每個月看多少本書？

How many movies do you see a year?
你一年看幾部電影？

Do you like playing chess?
你喜歡下棋嗎？

Do you like going to the movies?
你喜歡去看電影嗎？

Do you listen to the music at home?
你在家會聽音樂嗎？

⇨Do you work out?
你有在健身嗎？

⇨Are you good at singing?
你很會唱歌嗎？

⇨Are you interested in gardening?
你對園藝有興趣嗎？

⇨Are you good at dancing?
你擅長跳舞嗎？

•回答• •

⇨I like it very much.
我非常喜歡這件事。

⇨I'm crazy about it.
我對此很著迷。

⇨I'm very interested in it.
我對此很感興趣。

⇨It's OK.
還好。

⇨It's not bad.
還不錯。

▷I don't like it.
　我不喜歡它。

▷I hate it.
　我討厭它。

▷I have a strong dislike for it.
　我對此很不喜歡。

▷I can't stand it.
　我無法容忍。

● 說明興趣 ●　‧‧‧‧‧‧‧‧‧‧‧‧‧‧‧‧‧‧‧‧‧

▷I have a lot of interests.
　我的興趣廣泛。

▷My only hobby is reading.
　我唯一的興趣是閱讀。

▷Reading is my hobby.
　閱讀是我的興趣。

▷Traveling is one of my favorite hobbies.
　旅行是我最喜歡的興趣之一。

▷I'm good at dancing.
　我擅長跳舞。

▷I'm very interested in music.
我對音樂很有興趣。

▷I'm interested in reading novels.
我喜歡讀小說。

▷I'm interested in the internet.
我對網路很有興趣。

▷I'm very interested in photography.
我對攝影很有興趣。

▷I'm crazy about music.
我熱愛音樂。

▷I'm crazy about football.
我對足球很瘋狂。

▷I'm a drama fan.
我是個戲劇迷。

▷I'm taking dancing lessons.
我正在學跳舞。

▷I like bowling.
我喜歡打保齡球。

▷I like playing chess.
我喜歡下棋。

▷I like watching quiz shows on TV.
我喜歡看電視猜謎節目。

▷I like listening to classical music.
我喜歡聽古典音樂。

▷I like listening to pop music on FM.
我喜歡聽調頻電台的流行音樂。

▷I like listening to Enya's songs.
我喜歡聽恩雅的歌。

▷I like to play golf.
我喜歡打高爾夫。

▷I like to read romantic novels.
我喜歡讀浪漫小說。

▷I like to go to museums during vacation.
我喜歡在假日去逛博物館。

▷I love to go shopping.
我喜歡去購物。

▷I love to play guitar.
我喜歡彈吉他。

▷I enjoy collecting stamps.
我喜歡集郵。

▷ I enjoy listening to the music.
我喜歡聽音樂。

▷ I enjoy listening to the music on holidays.
我喜歡在假日聽音樂。

▷ I enjoy cable TV, too.
我也喜歡看有線電視的節目。

▷ I enjoy netsurfing almost every night.
我幾乎每天都喜歡上網逛逛。

▷ I play the guitar.
我會彈吉他。

▷ I can play the guitar a little.
我稍微會一點吉他。

▷ I think the film is wonderful.
我認為這部電影很棒。

▷ I admire Cely Dion.
我很景仰席林‧迪翁。

▷ I collect stamps as a hobby.
我的興趣是集郵。

▷ I read mysteries as a pastime.
我的嗜好是看神秘小說。

▷I go to dancing classes three times a month.
我每個月上三次跳舞課。

▷I often read a book before going to bed.
我睡前常看書。

▷I often enjoy video games at home.
我常在家打電動。

▷I often browse in bookstores.
我常在書店裡隨便瀏覽。

▷I often watch TV after taking a bath.
我常在洗澡後看電視

▷I usually go to a pub on weekends.
我週末通常會去酒吧。

▷I usually spend time with my family.
我通常週末的時候會陪伴家人。

▷I sometimes go to rock concerts.
我有時會去聽搖滾樂演唱會。

▷I sometimes spend all day on the Internet.
我時常整天上網。

▷I usually read novels when I have free time.
當我有空閒的時候，我經常讀小説。

❑ I always borrow books from the library.
我常到圖書館借書。

❑ I'd like to jog if I have time
如果有時間，我會慢跑。

❑ I'd like to jog to keep in good health.
為了維護健康，我會慢跑。

❑ I'd rather stay home and watch TV all day long.
我寧願一整天待在家裡看電視。

❑ I have been playing the piano since I was eight.
我從八歲的時候就開始彈鋼琴。

❑ I haven't been to the movie theaters lately.
最近我都沒去電影院了。

❑ I have no interest in sports.
我對運動沒什麼興趣。

❑ I'm poor at dancing.
我很不會跳舞。

❑ I'm poor at singing.
我很不會唱歌。

❑ I was deeply moved by Miss Potter.
《波特小姐》讓我很感動。

▷I was disappointed with Miss Potter.
　我對《波特小姐》感到失望。

▷One of my favorites book is Gone with the
　wind.
　我最愛的書籍之一《亂世佳人》。

▷Of all the moves stars, I like Tom Cruise the
　best.
　電影明星之中，我最喜歡湯姆‧克魯斯。

▷Roman Holiday is the best film I've ever seen.
　《羅馬假期》是我看過最棒的電影。

▷My favorite poet is Tim Washington.
　我喜歡的詩人是提姆‧華盛頓。

▷My favorite actor is Harrison Ford.
　我喜歡的演員是哈里遜‧福特。

▷My favorite painter is Picasso.
　我喜歡的畫家是畢卡索。

▷My favorite composer id Mozart.
　我喜歡的作曲家是莫札特。

實·用·會·話 1

A：Do you like tennis?

B：Yes, I do. I'm crazy about tennis.

A：Really? So am I. How about basketball?

B：I love basketball too. It's exciting.

A：你喜歡打網球嗎？

B：喜歡。我都迷上網球了。

A：真的嗎？我也是。籃球怎麼樣？

B：我也愛打籃球。它讓人興奮。

 深入分析

be crazy about 意即「對……著迷」，例如：

☑He is crazy about football games.

他對足球運動非常著迷。

☑Don't go crazy about computer games.

不要對電腦遊戲著迷。

實·用·會·話 2

A：Do you like the food in McDonald's?

B：Not really. How about you?

A：I love McDonald's. A big Mac hamburger, a glass of soda, and some French fries. I can never eat enough.

B：Have you heard of the term "junk food"?

A：What is junk food?

B：McDonald's food is junk food.

A：你喜歡麥當勞食品嗎？

B：不怎麼喜歡。你呢？

A：我喜歡。一個大的麥克漢堡，一杯汽水，再來一些法式油炸薯條。我是百吃不厭。

B：你聽說過「垃圾食物」嗎？

A：什麼是垃圾食物？

B：麥當勞就是垃圾食物。

 深入分析

1. junk food「垃圾食物」，指對健康無益的食品（food with little value to one's health）。

2. hear of 意思是「聽說」，例如：

☑ I have heard of him, but never seen him.
我聽說過他，但從沒見過。

☑ I've never heard of anyone doing a thing like that.
我從未聽過任何人做像這類的事。

實·用·會·話 3

A：你最喜歡什麼科目？

B：當然是英語。英語有趣而且有用。

A：你什麼時候開始對英語感興趣的？我以為你從來都不喜歡語言的。

B：哦，我不喜歡中文課，經典太多，背誦太多。英語課更是有趣。

A：What's your favorite subject at school?

B：English, of course. It's interesting and useful.

A：When did you become interested in it? I thought you never liked languages.

B：Well, I don't like the Chinese class, too much classics and too much recitation. The English class is more fun.

實·用·會·話 4

A：Great party, isn't it?

B：Yes, it is. The band is fantastic and so is the food.

A：Hi, my name is Bill Lin.

B：I'm Helen Kelly.

A：Would you like a drink, a glass of beer?

B：No, thanks. I don't like beer that much.

A：Well, how about a glass of wine?

B：That sounds good.

A：Red or white?

B：White, please. And dry. I like dry white wine.

A：So do I. Waiter, two glasses of white wine. Dry, please.

A：晚會棒極了，不是嗎？

B：是啊。樂隊棒極了，餐點也是。

A：你好，我叫比爾・林。

B：我是海倫・凱蕾。

A：來杯飲料怎麼樣，啤酒？

B：不，謝謝。我不太喜歡啤酒。

A：那麼來葡萄酒如何？

B：好啊！

A：紅葡萄酒還是白葡萄酒？

B：請來杯白葡萄酒吧，不甜的。我喜歡不甜的白葡萄酒。

A：我也是。服務員，請來兩杯白葡萄酒，要不含糖的。

 深入分析

在西方的飲料中，把不含糖分的叫做 dry，例如我們說「乾白葡萄酒」是 dry white grape wine，而「乾啤酒」則是 dry beer。

實·用·會·話 5

A：Bob, do you have any hobbies?

B：Yes, reading is my hobby.

A：What kind of books do you like to read?

B：All kinds of books.

When I was a kid in elementary school, I enjoyed reading fables and science fiction.

When I became a teenager at high school, I was interested in detective and mystery stories.

Now I like reading romance.

A：Are you in love?

B：Why?

A：They say only those who are in love like
　　to read romance stories.

B：Well, maybe they're right.

A：鮑勃，你有什麼嗜好？

B：閱讀是我的愛好。

A：你喜歡讀什麼書？

B：什麼書我都愛讀。

　　上小學的時候，我喜歡讀寓言和科幻。

　　到了中學，我對偵探和神秘小說感興趣。

　　現在我喜歡讀浪漫小說。

A：你在戀愛吧？

B：怎麼說？

A：人家說只有那些在戀愛的人喜歡讀浪漫小
　　說。

B：噢，有點道理。

 深入分析

　　enjoy 後面的受詞只能用名詞、代名詞、反
義代名詞和動名詞，不能用不定詞，例如：

☑enjoy ⎰ listening to the music 喜歡聽音樂
　　　　⎱ reading books 喜歡讀書
　　　　⎱ playing baseball 喜歡打棒球

《片語》
enjoy oneself 玩得開心
enjoy one's holiday 假日玩得開心

實·用·會·話 6

A：Are you watching the TV series now shown on Channel 8?

B：No, I haven't been watching it.
I don't care much for soap operas. They are just not my cup of tea.

A：They are too confusing. But a lot of people enjoy watching them. They say soaps are entertaining.

B：Yes, only two kinds of people like watching soap operas.

A：Who are they?

B：Those who don't have to work and those who have too much work.
The former need something to help them kill time and the latter need something to take their minds off work.

A：You are exactly right. I prefer news and science programs.

B：Me, too. I think they are both informative and entertaining.

A：你現在收看第八頻道的電視連續劇嗎？

B：我沒看。
我不太喜歡肥皂劇，不合我胃口。

A：這種劇太讓人糊塗了。但很多人卻喜歡看。
他們說肥皂劇讓人得以消遣。

B：只有兩種人喜歡看肥皂劇。

A：哪些人呢？

B：那些沒有工作的和那些工作過度的。
前者需要消磨時光，後者需要讓自己忘掉工作。

A：對極了。我更喜歡新聞和科技節目。

B：我也是。我覺得這兩種節目既有資訊性又有消遣性。

 深入分析

1. not my cup of tea 意思是「不對我的口味、不是我所喜歡的」，例如：

☑Novels by J. K. Rowling are not my cup of tea.

J. K.羅琳寫的小說我不喜歡。

2. kill time 字面意思是「殺死時間」，引申為「消磨時間」、「打發時間」，例如：

☑They played cards to kill the time.

他們打撲克牌消磨時間。

3. take one's minds off 意思是「放鬆」，例如：

☑I often listen to light music to take my mind off.

我常聽輕音樂來放鬆自己。

1. How many legs do horses have?

   馬有幾條腿？

2. When are people smartest?

   什麼時候人最聰明？

3. I have a tree in my hand. What kind of tree is it?

   我的手上有棵樹，是什麼樹？

1. Six legs–forelegs in front and two in back.

   有六條腿,前面有前腿,後面有兩條腿。

   原來如此

   forelegs 發音與 four legs 相似。

2. When it's sunny, because everything's brighter then.

   當天氣晴朗的時候,因為這時候萬物都更明亮。

   原來如此

   bright 除了是「光亮」之外,也是「聰明」的意思。

3. It's palm.

   是手掌。

   原來如此

   palm 除了是「手掌」,也是「棕櫚科植物」的意思。

Unit 12

道歉

• 道歉 • • • • • • • • • • • • • • • •

▷Excuse me.
借過。對不起。（在此非道歉之意）

▷Sorry for being late.
對不起，我遲到了。

▷Excuse my interrupting you.
對不起，打擾你們。

▷Will you excuse us?
可以讓我們失陪一下嗎？

▷Sorry for interrupting your talk, but I have something important to tell you.
抱歉打斷各位的談話，不過我有重要的事要告訴你們。

▷Sorry.
抱歉。（道歉之意）

▷I'm sorry.
抱歉。

▷I'm very sorry about that.
為此我很抱歉。

▷I am terribly sorry.

我很抱歉。

⮩I am awfully sorry.
我很抱歉。

⮩Sorry! Did I step on you?
對不起！我是不是踩到你了？

⮩Sorry, David, I have to cancel our meeting.
抱歉，大衛，我得取消會議。

⮩Sorry, I can't do it by myself.
對不起，我沒有辦法一個人完成。

⮩Sorry I can't stop. I have no time.
很抱歉，我不能停下。我沒有時間。

⮩Sorry, I didn't catch you.
抱歉，我沒有聽懂。

⮩Sorry, I don't know.
對不起，我不清楚。

⮩Sorry, I kept you waiting.
對不起，讓你久等了。

⮩I am sorry to bother you.
對不起給你添麻煩。

➡ I am sorry to bother you with all this work.
很抱歉麻煩你做這些事。

➡ I am sorry to disappoint you.
很抱歉讓你失望。

➡ I am sorry to disturb you.
對不起,打擾你了。

➡ I am sorry to let you down.
對不起讓你失望了。

➡ Sorry to have kept you waiting.
抱歉讓你久等。

➡ Pardon?
你說什麼?

➡ I beg your pardon. I suppose I should have knocked.
抱歉,我想我應該先敲一下門的。

➡ I apologized to you.
我向你道歉。

➡ Please forgive me.
請原諒我。

➡ Please accept my apology.

請接受我的道歉。

▷Will you forgive me?
你能原諒我嗎？

▷I'm sorry for what I have said to you.
我為我向你説過的話表示道歉。

▷I'm sorry. I didn't mean to hurt your feelings.
對不起。我沒有傷害你的意思。

▷I must apologize for ....
我必須為……而道歉。

▷I'd like to make an apology for ...
我想為……而道歉。

▷I'm afraid I've brought you too much trouble.
我想我已經給你帶來了太多的麻煩。

回覆道歉

▷That's OK/all right.
沒關係。

▷It's nothing.
沒什麼。

▷It's OK.

沒關係。

⇨Never mind.
不要在意。

⇨It doesn't matter.
不要緊。

⇨It's no trouble at all.
一點也不麻煩的。

⇨It's not your fault.
不是你的錯。

⇨It's no big deal.
沒什麼大不了的。

⇨Everything will be fine.
凡事都會順利。

⇨No problem.
沒啥問題啦！

⇨Forget it.
算了。

⇨Don't let it worry you.
別為此事擔心。

⮕I quite understand.
　我非常理解。

⮕Never mind. It doesn't really matter.
　別介意。真的沒關係。

⮕Please don't worry about that.
　請別為此事擔心。

實·用·會·話 1

A：Excuse me for interrupting.

B&C：Yes, what is it?

A：Would you please fill out this form? It's
　　for our records.

(B&C each fills out a form and gives it to A)

A：Thank you. Sorry for the interruption.

B&C：That's all right.

（B和C正在說話）

A：對不起，打擾一下。

B&C：什麼事？

A：請你們填這張表好嗎？這是我們存檔用的。

（B和C 每人填一張交給A）

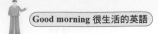

A：謝謝。對不起打斷了你們的談話。

B&C：沒關係。

深入分析

> fill out 是個動詞片語，意思是「填寫（表格）」、「長胖」，例如：
>
> ☑ You'll have to fill out these forms before getting the loan.
>
> 獲得貸款前，要填寫這些表格。
>
> ☑ Her cheeks have filled out.
>
> 她的臉頰豐腴起來了。

實·用·會·話 2

A：Excuse me, Mr. Smith. Would you please lend me your bike?

B：Certainly, here you are.

A：Thank you. I just want to go to the hospital.

B：There's no hurry. Take your time. I'm not using it now.

A：對不起，史密斯先生，請把自行車借給我用一下行嗎？

B：當然可以，自行車在這裏。

A：謝謝，我想去趟醫院。

B：別著急，慢點兒。我現在也不用它。

 深入分析

take you time 意思是「放鬆點、別著急」，例如：

☑Take your time, the meeting won't start till five.

別著急，會議五點鐘才開始呢。

實·用·會·話 3

A：Excuse me. Would you mind giving Miss Jones a message?

B：I'll be glad to.

A：Please tell her the computer class is not at seven thirty, but at seven tomorrow morning.

B：All right.

A：Thank you. And please don't forget.

B：No, I won't.

A：勞駕！你能給瓊斯小姐捎個口信嗎？

B：我很樂意。

A：請轉告她明早的電腦課是七點而不是七點
　　半。

B：好的。

A：謝謝。請別忘了。

B：我不會忘的。

深入分析

1. Would you mind ...? 「你介意…嗎？」

這一句型用來表示客氣的請求，後接動名
詞的形式，例如：

☑Would you mind letting me pass?
你不介意讓我通過吧？

☑Would you mind passing me the salt?
能把鹽遞給我嗎？

2. I'll be glad to 「我很願意」

通常用來表達樂意幫助別人或去做某人所
要求的事，例如：

☑ "Could you help me with my English?"
「你能幫我學英語嗎？」

☑ "I'll be glad to."
「我很樂意（幫你）。」

實·用·會·話 4

A：I'm terribly sorry, John. I lost your magazine.

B：It doesn't matter . It was a back number anyway.

A：I've tried to find another copy but couldn't find one.

B：Don't worry about it. I don't need it any more.

A：真是非常抱歉，約翰，我把你的雜誌弄丟了。

B：沒關係，反正是本過期雜誌。

A：我試圖找一本，但沒能找到。

B：不用擔心，我也用不著它了。

 深入分析

　　terribly是副詞，表「非常地」的意思，程度比 very 更強烈，例如：

☑I've been terribly worried about you all day.

　　我一整天都非常地擔心你。

☑We were terribly lucky to find you here.

　　我們很幸運能在此找到你。

實·用·會·話 5

(On the phone)

A：Hello, Henry. It's Mary.

B：Hello, Mary. Good morning.

A：I'm very sorry, Henry. I'm not feeling well. I don't think I can go to the party tonight.

B：Oh, dear. I'm sorry to hear that.

A：I hope I'm not upsetting you too much.

B：Oh, well, I understand. Don't worry about the party.

（電話中）

A：喂，亨利，我是瑪麗。

B：喂，瑪麗，早安。

A：十分抱歉，亨利。我身體不太舒服。我看今晚的晚會我無法參加了。

B：哎呀！這太遺憾了。

A：我希望不致於使你過分失望。

B：噢，我能理解的。別為晚會的事擔心了。

感謝

• 表示感謝 • • • • • • • • • • • • • • • • • •

⇨Thanks.
多謝。

⇨Thanks a lot.
多謝了。

⇨Thank you.
謝謝！

⇨Thank you so much.
非常感激。

⇨Thank you anyway.
還是要感謝你。

⇨Thanks to you and your staff.
謝謝你及你的員工。

⇨Thanks for your kindness.
謝謝你的好心。

⇨Thanks for saying so.
感謝你這麼説。

⇨Thanks for asking me out.
感謝你約我出來。

⇨Thanks for cheering me up.
感謝你鼓勵我。

⇨Thanks for asking.
謝謝邀請。

⇨Thank you for your help.
謝謝你的幫忙。

⇨Thank you very much.
非常感謝你。

⇨Thank you for your time.
感謝撥冗。

⇨Thank you for your patient.
謝謝你的耐心。

⇨Thank you for the delicious dishes.
感謝你的佳餚。

⇨Thank you for everything.
謝謝所有的事。

⇨Thank you for all you have done for me.
謝謝你為我做的一切。

⇨Thank you for coming.
謝謝你的來訪。

▷Thank you for calling.
　謝謝你打電話。

▷Thank you for listening.
　感謝你聽我傾訴。

▷Thank you for telling me.
　謝謝你告訴我。

▷Thank you for helping me.
　謝謝你幫我。

▷Thank you for making me a mom.
　感謝你讓我成為一名母親。

▷Thank you for making me stronger.
　感謝你讓我更強壯。

▷Thank you for making me feel important.
　感謝你讓我覺得好多了。

▷Thank you for making me feel needed.
　感謝你讓我覺得被需求。

▷Thank you for making me feel so loved.
　感謝你讓我覺得被愛。

▷Thank you for making me feel confident.
　感謝你讓我覺得有自信。

✑Thank you for making me breakfast every morning.
感謝你每天幫我做早餐。

✑Thank you for making me become interested in English.
感謝你讓我變得對英文有興趣。

✑Thank you for making me feel so comfortable.
感謝你讓我覺得自在舒服。

✑Thank you for making me so welcome here.
謝謝你讓我覺得在這裡是受歡迎的。

✑Thank you for making me feel welcome and comfortable.
感謝你讓我覺得自在舒服和受歡迎。

✑Thank you for making me feel safe and wealthy.
感謝你讓我覺得安全及富裕。

✑Thank you for making me calm down in time!
感謝你讓我及時冷靜下來。

✑Thank you for making me one of your members.

感謝你讓我成為你們的一員。

⇨Thank you for letting me know I wasn't the only one.
感謝你讓我知道我不是唯一的一個人。

⇨Thank you for making me feel so special on my birthday.
感謝你讓我在我生日時感覺這麼特別。

⇨Thank you for remembering my birthday.
感謝記得我的生日。

⇨Much appreciated.
非常感激。

⇨I appreciate your help.
感謝幫忙。

⇨I appreciate your kindness.
感謝你的關心。

⇨It's really helpful.
很有幫助。

⇨I really appreciate it.
我真的很感謝。

⇨I can't thank you enough.

真不知道該如何感謝你。

▷I have no words to thank you.
不知說什麼才能感謝您。

▷You have been very helpful.
你真的幫了大忙。

▷That's very nice of you.
你真好。

▷That's very kind of you.
你真好。

▷How kind of you.
你真好。

• 回覆感謝 • •

▷You are welcome.
不客氣。

▷It's OK.
沒關係。

▷Not at all.
完全不會。

▷No problem.

一點也不（麻煩）。

⮑Don't mention it.
　　不客氣。

⮑Don't worry about it.
　　別這麼説。

⮑It was no trouble.
　　不麻煩。

⮑My pleasure.
　　我的榮幸。

⮑You should.
　　你是應該（説謝謝）！

⮑Sure.
　　當然（要説謝謝）。

實·用·會·話 1

A：Would you help me move this box?

B：Yes. Oh, this box is very heavy.

A：Yes, it is. Now, I have to wrap the box.

B：Let's put the box down on the table.

A：Fine. Get me a hammer, will you?

B：Yes, I will. Here you are.

A：你幫我移動一下這個箱子，好嗎？

B：好的，哦，這箱子可真重。

A：是啊。現在我要把箱子封起來。

B：把箱子放在桌子上吧。

A：好。幫我拿個錘子，好嗎？

B：好。給你。

實·用·會·話 2

A：Would you mind helping me hang up this picture?

B：Of course not. I'll be glad to.

A：Hold it straight, while I put in the nail.

B：OK.

A：There. How does that look? Do I have it straight?

B：Yes, it's straight.

A：你介意幫我把這幅畫掛起來嗎？

B：當然願意效勞。

A：請把畫扶正。我要釘釘子。

B：好啊！

A：喂，看看怎麼樣？掛正了嗎?

B：是的，掛正了。

 深入分析

　　Of course not.「當然不。」

因為問題是問 Would you mind...（你介意…
嗎），所以回答 Of course not 表示「不介意
做…」之意。

　　另一種 would you mind 的問句的回答方
式，若表示願意，也可以說：not at all（完
全不介意），例如：

☑ "Would you mind closing the window for
　me?"

　「你介意幫我關窗戶嗎？」

　"Of course not."

　「好啊！（我不介意幫你關窗戶）」

　"No, not at all."

　「好，我不介意。」

實·用·會·話 3

A：Oh, Jim. Would you do me a favor?

B：Why not.

A：Will you type this letter for me?

B：Certainly. When do you want it?

A：Tomorrow is OK?

B：I think that will be all right.

A：Thank you very much.

B：Don't mention it.

A：噢，吉姆，幫我個忙，可以嗎？

B：當然可以啦。

A：能幫我把這封信打字好嗎？

B：當然可以。你什麼時候要？

A：明天行嗎？

B：我想可以。

A：那就太謝謝你啦！

B：不用客氣。

 深入分析

　　why not 這裏相當於 of course/ok，表示「願意、為何不」的肯定回答，而不是表示疑問。

☑ "Would you give me a hand?"

　　「可以幫我忙嗎？」

　　"Why not."

　　「好啊。」

實·用·會·話 4

A：Say, Henry, I was wondering if you could help me with my English.

B：My pleasure. When?

A：How about tomorrow afternoon?

B：I'm sorry, but I shall not be free then. What about this evening?

A：All right. This evening is fine. See you then.

B：See you.

A：喂，亨利，你能不能輔導一下我的英語。

B：當然可以啦。什麼時候開始呢？

A：明天下午怎麼樣？

B：對不起，明天下午我沒空。今晚怎麼樣？

A：行，那就今晚吧。晚上見。

B：晚上見。

深入分析

1. I was wondering if... 是 I wonder if...更委
   婉的說法，意思是「不知你（能否）
   ……」如：

☑ I was wondering if you could help me mail
   this letter?

   不知道你能否幫我寄這封信。

2. How about... 和 What about... 都是用來表
   示向對方提出建議，意思是「……可以
   嗎？／行嗎？」，例如：

☑ How about the day after tomorrow?

   後天行嗎？

☑ What about the Grand Hotel?

   圓山飯店可以嗎？

請求幫助

• 要求 •

⮑ Give me hand, please.
請幫我一下。

⮑ I need help.
我需要幫助。

⮑ Help!
救命啊！

⮑ Can I ask a favor?
我可以要求幫忙嗎？

⮑ Can you ...?
你能……嗎？

⮑ Would/Will you please ...?
請你……好嗎？

⮑ Would you mind (doing) ...?
你介意……嗎？

⮑ Do me a favor and close the window, please.
請幫我個忙把窗戶關上。

⮑ I wonder if you could ....
不知道你能否……。

▷I was wondering if you could ....
不知你能不能……。

• 回答 •

▷Certainly.
當然。

▷Yes, of course.
當然。

▷Ok.
好。

▷Sure.
好啊！

▷How may I help?
需要我幫忙嗎？

▷What is it?
（要幫）什麼？

▷What is it about?
是關於什麼事？

▷No problem.
沒問題。

⮑Go ahead.

說吧。（要幫什麼？）

⮑With pleasure.

好啊！

⮑Leave it to me.

交給我來辦就好。

⮑You are the boss.

你是老闆。（你說了就算。）

⮑I will be happy to.

我很樂意。

⮑I will do it for you.

我會幫你做。

⮑No, not at all.

好啊！

⮑What do you want me to do?

你要我做什麼？

⮑I'd be glad/delighted to.

我很高興／樂意（去做）。

⮑I'd like to, but I have to go to the station right now.

我倒是想去做，但我必須馬上去一趟車站。

⇨Sorry, I can't help you.
抱歉，我不能幫你。

⇨Sorry, I am in the middle of something.
抱歉，我正在忙。

⇨I can't help you at the moment.
我現在不能幫你。

⇨I can't do anything now.
我現在不能做任何事。

⇨I have other business to take care.
我有事要忙。

⇨Sorry, not right now.
抱歉，現在不行。

⇨Ask someone else.
去要求別人吧。

⇨I am afraid I couldn't.
我恐怕不行。

實·用·會·話 1

A：Hello, Tom. Would you do me a favor?

B：Yes.

A：Mail this letter for me on your way to the bookstore, please?

B：Sure. Do you want it to be registered?

A：Yes, I think so. There are some pictures in it. It would be great pity if they were lost.

B：Yes. I will be glad to be of help.

A：Thanks.

B：You're welcome.

A：湯姆，你好。幫一個忙，好嗎？

B：你說吧！

A：你在去書店的路上幫我把這封信寄了，好嗎？

B：可以。你想寄掛號信嗎？

A：是的，我是這樣認為。信裏有幾張照片。要是丟了，實在可惜。

B：是的。我很樂意幫忙。

A：謝謝。

B：不客氣。

深入分析

> do somebody a favor 意思是「幫某人忙」，
> 例如：
>
> ☑Please do me a favor and carry this luggage
> to the third floor.
>
> 請幫我個忙，將行李搬到三樓。
>
> ☑Do me a favor, please.
>
> 請幫我忙。

實·用·會·話 2

A：May I borrow your dictionary for a couple of days?

B：It depends on when.

A：Oh, just over the weekends. I won't keep
 it for long.

B：Yes, I guess that would be all right.

A：Thank you.

B：Don't mention it.

A：我可以借你的詞典用幾天嗎？

B：看什麼時候借。

A：噢，就這個週末。我不會借太久的。

B：行，我想可以。

A：謝謝。

B：不客氣。

深入分析

1. a couple of = several 意思是「幾個」而不
   是「一對」之意。但 a couple 單用時則表
   示「一對（夫妻）」，例如：

☑ They are a couple.

   他們是一對。

☑ The young couple had a quarrel yesterday.

   年輕的夫妻昨天吵了一架。

☑ He went to Canada a couple of weeks ago.

   他幾週前去了加拿大。

2. depend (on) 意思是「取決於」，例如：

☑ "Is there a meeting tomorrow?"

   「明天開會嗎？」

☑ "It depends."

   「不一定。」

☑ It depends on you.

   這就取決於你了。

3. Don't mention it. 用來回答別人的感謝，意
   思是「別客氣、不用謝謝」。

☑ "Thank you for your help."

「謝謝你的幫忙。」

"Don't mention it."

「不用客氣。」

實·用·會·話 3

A：Would you please do me a favor, David?

B：Of course.

A：Could you lend me your camera?

B：Sure, here you are.

A：That's very kind of you.

A：大衛，幫個忙，好嗎？

B：當然可以。

A：你能把相機借給我用嗎？

B：可以，給你。

Λ：你真好。

實·用·會·話 4

A：Would you help me for a minute, please?

B：Yes. What do you want me to do?

A：Could you hold these packages while I
   look for the key to the door?

B：I'd be glad to.

A：請問，你能幫我一會兒嗎？

B：可以。你想要我做什麼？

A：你能幫我把這些包包拿著嗎？我來找一下門
　　的鑰匙。

B：我很樂意。

深入分析

key to the door「門的鑰匙」
意思是「門的鑰匙」不是 key of the door。
這種表示所屬關係方法比較特殊，類似的表
達有：
☑answer to the question
　問題的答案
☑entrance to the cinema
　戲院的門口
☑solution to the problem
　解決問題的方法
☑bridge to knowledge
　知識的橋等。

提供幫助

•問句•••••••••••••••••••••••••••

▷Is there anything I can do (get/buy) for you?
有什麼需要我幫你做（拿／買）的嗎？

▷Let me help you.
我來幫你。

▷Let me give you a hand.
我來幫你吧！

▷Would you like me to ...?
你想讓我……嗎？

▷Why not use my bike?
何不用我的自行車呢？

▷Can I get a taxi for you?
我來給你叫輛計程車吧！

▷Shall I help you to make the bed?
我來幫你整理床吧！

▷I can help you.
我可以幫你。

▷Do you need help?
你需要幫忙嗎？

➪How may I help you?
　有需要我幫忙的嗎？

➪Is there anything I can do for you?
　有需要我幫忙的嗎？

➪Anything wrong?
　怎麼啦？

・回答・ •

➪It's very kind of you.
　你真好。

➪Yes, please.
　是的。（我需要幫忙）。

➪Wouldn't that be too much bother?
　那不是太麻煩你了嗎？

➪Please don't bother. Thank you all the same.
　不麻煩你了。還是得謝謝你。

➪Please don't bother.
　請不必這麼麻煩。

➪I can handle wih it by myself.
　我可以自己來。

▷I can do it by myself.
　我可以自己來。

▷I can manage it.
　我可以自己來（不需要幫助）。

▷I can manage all right.
　我可以自己來。

實·用·會·話 1

A：Oh, that's too bad! I've got a flat tire .

B：Are you in a hurry?

A：Yes. I have to go to the hospital to see David.

B：Then why don't you ride my bike there while I get yours repaired?

A：That's very kind of you. Thank you very much.

B：You are welcome. Please say hello to him for me.

A：呀，真糟糕！爆胎了。

B：你有急事嗎？

A：是的，我得去醫院看大衛。

B：不如你騎我的車吧，我把你的車拿去修理。

A：你真是太好了。非常感謝。

B：別客氣。請代我向他問好。

深入分析

> Why not... 和 Why don't you... 表達相同的
> 含義，意思是「何不……呢？」，表示向他
> 人提出建議，例如：
> ☑ Why not go with me?
> =Why don't you go with me?
> 何不和我一起去呢？

實·用·會·話 2

A：What's the matter with your foot?

B：I fell down the steps just now.

A：Let me have a look.

(A feels B's ankle.).

B：Ouch, that hurts.

A：Would you like me to take you to the hospital? You might have broken a bone.

B：It's very kind of you. But someone is

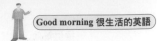

getting a car for me. Thank you just the same.

A：你的腳怎麼啦？

B：我剛從樓梯摔下來。

A：讓我看看。

（A 摸 B 的腳踝）

B：哎喲！疼啊！

A：我帶你上醫院吧！你可能骨折了。

B：你真好，但有人幫我叫車了，還是要謝謝你。

深入分析

What's the matter with = What's wrong with...? 意思是「…… 出了什麼問題/毛病？」，例如：

☑You look listless. What's wrong with you?
你看起來無精打采的，有什麼不舒服嗎？

實·用·會·話 3

A：Is there anything I can do to help you?

B：Yes, please. I'd like some help carrying these bags.

A：All right.

B：Thank you.

A：You are welcome.

A：有什麼事需要我幫忙的嗎？

B：好的，那就麻煩你啦。我想請你幫我提一下
這些手提包。

A：好的。

B：謝謝啦！

A：別客氣！

實·用·會·話 4

A：Let me help you with the suitcase, Alice.
Your hands are full.

B：I can manage all right, Henry. Thanks
just the same.

A：Come on, hand it over. It's pretty far to
the station.

B：Well, if you insist.

A：讓我來幫你提箱子吧，艾麗絲。你手上拿的
東西太多了。

B：我自己能做到，亨利。儘管如此，還是要謝

謝你。

A：來吧，交給我吧。離火車站還相當遠呢！

B：好吧，假如你堅持一定要這樣的話。

 深入分析

> I can manage all right. 意思是「我能應付
> 得了」，例如：
> ☑I can manage without his help.
> 沒有他的幫助，我也能應付得了。

實·用·會·話 5

A：May I help you with your parcels?

B：Thank you. You take this one and I'll take the other one.

A：It's so heavy. What is it?

B：They're new books sent by our friends.

A：Good, we need them.

B：Here we are. Thank you very much.

A：Not at all.

A：需要我幫你拿包裹嗎？

B：謝謝。你拿這個包裹，我拿那個包裹。

A：很重呢，是什麼東西啊？

B：是我們的朋友寄來的新書。

A：好，我們正需要書。

B：到了，太謝謝你啦！

A：不用謝。

深入分析

　　May I help you with your parcels? 「我可以幫你拿包裹嗎？」

　　help sb. with sth. 意思是「幫助某人做某事」，例如：

☑She often helps her mother with housework.
她經常幫她媽媽做家務。

實·用·會·話 6

A：Can I help you, sir?

B：Yes, please. I need a taxi to go to the rail-way station.

A：Oh, there happens to have a taxi. Have you got any luggage?

B：Yes, two suitcases in my room.

A：OK. Let's go to your room to get your luggage first.

B：Should I pay for the luggage?

A：No. You just pay for the taxi fares.

B：Thank you for your help.

A：Don't mention it.

A：我可以幫你嗎，先生？

B：好的。 我需要一輛計程車送我到火車站。

A：哎呀，我的計程車正好就停在這兒。你有行
李嗎？

B：有啊。兩個手提箱，在我房間裏。

A：沒問題。那我們先到你房間拿行李吧！

B：要付費嗎？

A：不用，你付計程車費就行了。

B：謝謝你幫忙。

A：不客氣！

 深入分析

　　happen (to) 在這裏的意思是「碰巧」，例
如：

☑It happened that I was passing that street.
　碰巧我路過那條街道。

☑It happened that someone called on me.
　碰巧有人來找我。

Unit **16**

同情

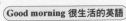

●你可以這麼表達● ● ● ● ● ● ● ● ● ● ● ● ● ● ● ● ● ● ● ●

⇨How unfortunate!
　多不幸啊！

⇨That's too bad!
　太糟了！

⇨That's a pity.
　真可惜！

⇨What a shame!
　真可惜！

⇨How sad/terrible/awful to hear Tom's accident!
　聽到湯姆的事故，真是太令人覺得悲傷／可怕了。

⇨What bad luck!
　多壞的運氣！

⇨I'm sorry to hear that.
　聽到這件事我很難過。

⇨I'm sorry to hear..., what bad luck!
　聽到……我很難過，多壞的運氣呀！

⇨I'm sorry that you lost your job.

你失業了我真難過。

⇨I'm sorry/shocked to learn that you'll be leaving the company.

得知你將離開公司我很難過／震驚。

⇨I feel very/terribly sorry for you.

我為你感到難過。

⇨I know how you must feel.

我理解你的感受。

〈• 你可以這麼回答 •〉• • • • • • • • • • • • • •

⇨Thank you.

謝謝你。

⇨Thank you for asking.

謝謝關心。

⇨Thank you for your concern.

謝謝你的關心。

⇨Thank you so much for your concern.

非常感謝你的關心。

⇨I appreciate your kindness.

我感謝你的好意。

⟡I'm deeply moved/touched. Thank you.
  我深受感動。謝謝你。

⟡It's very nice/kind of you to offer/to help.
  你來幫我真是太好了。

實·用·會·話 1

A : I was told that Tom's house was robbed.

B : Yes. It happened last night.

A : How shocking! What did the robbers get away with?

B : Three thousand dollars in cash and four thousand in current deposit.

A : What a shame! Tom must be feeling miserable. Let's call him and see if we can be of any help.

A：我聽說湯姆的房子遭小偷了。

B：是的,昨天夜裏發生的。

A：太嚇人了!盜賊拿走了什麼?

B：三千元現金,四千元的活期存摺。

A：真可惜!湯姆一定感到很難過。我們打電話給他吧,看看能幫他做點什麼。

深入分析

1. How shocking!意思是「太嚇人了!」或者「真令人震驚!」,表示說話者的震驚,例如:

☑How shocking! He was murdered last night.
太嚇人了!他昨晚被謀殺了。

2. What a shame! 意思是「真可惜!」,表示說話者的遺憾,例如:

☑What a shame! He hasn't passed the exam.
真可惜!他沒有通過這次考試。

實·用·會·話 2

A: Mary, I was really shocked to hear about your husband's accident! I'm really sorry.

B: Thank, Jenny. We're just thankful that it wasn't any worse than it was.

A: Please let me know if there's anything I can do. I'll be glad to take care of the kids while you go to the hospital.

B: Thanks so much, Jenny. I might need

your help tomorrow if you don't mind.

A：Not at all. And please tell John we're all thinking about him and wishing him a fast recovery.

B：That's really kind of you.

A：瑪麗，聽到你丈夫出了事故時，我真是嚇壞了！我實在是感到遺憾。

B：謝謝，珍妮。所幸的是已經轉危為安了。

A：如果我能為你做點什麼，請告訴我。你去醫院時，我會很樂意照顧孩子們。

B：太感謝了，珍妮，如果你不介意的話，我明天可能需要你幫忙。

A：一點也不（介意）。請轉告約翰我們都很想他，希望他早日恢復健康。

B：你真是太好了。

 深入分析

1. And please tell John we're all thinking about him and wishing him a fast recovery. 意思是「請轉告約翰我們都很想他，希望他早日恢復健康。」這句話表達了對遇到車禍的友人的復原祝福，例如：

☑We are all thinking about our teacher and wishing her a fast recovery.

我們都很想念我們的老師,並希望她早日康復。

2. It's really nice (kind) of you.意思是「你真是太好了。」表達了說話者的感激之情,例如:

☑ "Let me help you with it."

「讓我來幫你的忙。」

"It's really nice of you."

「你真是太好了。」

實·用·會·話 3

A : Sophia, I'm deeply sorry to hear about your grandmother's death. She was such a wonderful person, and we all loved her so much.

B : Thank you for your sympathy, Linda. She loved you, Linda.

A : Please accept my condolences. Let me know if there is anything I can do for you.

B : Thanks for the flowers. You are really thoughtful.

A : Well, I'll let you go now. There are a lot of other people waiting to talk to you.
I'll see you tomorrow at the funeral service.

B : Thanks again, Linda, for coming.

A : 蘇菲亞，聽到你祖母的事，我深感遺憾。她曾是這麼好的人，而且我們都如此愛她。

B : 謝謝你的同情，琳達。她是這麼地愛你，琳達。

A : 在此謹致慰問之意，如果我能為你做什麼，請告訴我。

B : 謝謝你帶來的花。你真是太周到了。

A : 哦，我不耽擱你了。許多人在等著和你說話。
明天葬禮上見吧！

B : 琳達，我為你的慰問再次表示感謝。

深入分析

　　You arc rcally thoughtful.意思是「你真是太周到了。」非常適合回應對方的慰問，如：

☑Thank you for your gifts. You are really thoughtful.

　謝謝你的禮物。你真是太周到了。

實·用·會·話 4

A：Do you remember the new apartment John and Mary just moved into last month?

B：Why do you say that?

A：Well, it turns out it's almost a twenty-minute walk to the nearest bus stop.

B：How terrible! They thought they were nearer to the company.

A：That is not all. No stores are open in the neighborhood.

　　That means they have to buy food and supplies from downtown.

B：Oh, no.

A：What is even worse, gas hasn't been installed as promised yet.

B：That's really trouble.

Cooking without a gas stove is most inconvenient. We did that for almost a year too.

It's unfortunate they have all those problems.

A：Let's hope things will get better.

A：你還記得約翰和瑪麗上個月剛搬進去的新公寓嗎？

B：怎麼說起了這個？

A：噢，原來它離最近的汽車站幾乎要走二十分鐘。

B：太糟了！他們原以為離公司更近了。

A：還不止這些呢，附近也沒有商店。

這就是說他們得從市中心買食品和日用品。

B：哦，怎麼是這樣！

A：更糟糕的是，瓦斯並沒有像當初答應的那樣得到安裝。

B：那真是麻煩透了。

沒有瓦斯做飯就太不方便了。我們也有將近
一年都是那樣過來的。

那些問題他們都碰到了，實在不幸。

A：我們希望事情將會轉好。

深入分析

1. turn out 意思是「證明為、結果是」。例
   如：

☑ Everything turned out well.

結果一切都很好。

☑ It turned out he's a robber.

結果他是一個搶劫犯。

2. what is even worse 意思是「更糟糕的是
   ……」，置於句首，作為副詞片語。例
   如：

☑ What's even worse, they have no enough
   money.

更糟糕的是，他們沒有足夠的錢。

☑ What's even worse, Mary knows nothing
   about it.

更糟糕的是，瑪麗對此一無所知。

實·用·會·話 5

A : I'm so upset, Jean. I didn't get the promotion.

B : I'm really sorry to hear that. I can't believe this, Bill.
You are the best in the office. If anyone deserved it, you did.

A : Thanks for your understanding, Jean. I really did think I was going to get it. That's why it hurts me so much.

B : Don't let it get you down. There'll be other promotions.

A：我很難過，琴。我沒有得到升職。

B：實在是遺憾，我簡直不能相信，比爾。
你是這個辦公室最好的，如果有什麼人該升遷的話，那就是你。

A：感謝你的理解，琴。我原先真的想我會升遷的，這就是我受到如此傷害的原因。

B：不要因此而氣餒。會有其他升遷機會的。

深入分析

　　get sb. down 意思是「使某人感到沮喪」，
例如：

☑Don't let the failure get you down.
　不要讓這次的失敗使你沮喪。

☑The bad news got them down.
　壞消息使他們很沮喪。

實·用·會·話 6

A：Tom, I'm really sorry to hear that your
　　bike was stolen.

　　Did you hear anything from the police?

B：Not yet.

A：Well, if you need to go somewhere, you
　　are welcome to use mine.

B：Thanks, John. That's very nice of you.

A：湯姆，聽說你的自行車被偷了，我實在為你
　　難過。

　　警方那兒有什麼消息嗎？

B：還沒有。

A：哦，如果你要去什麼地方，你可以用我的。

B：謝謝，約翰。你真好。

深入分析

1. be welcome to do sth.意思是「可隨意做某事、可隨意取用某物」如：

☑You are welcome to use my bike.

你可以用我的自行車。

2. welcome 還可用這樣的表達：welcome sb. to some place「歡迎某人至某地」，例如：

☑Welcome home!

歡迎回家！

☑Welcome back

歡迎回來！

☑Welcome to our school.

歡迎蒞臨我們的學校。

Unit **17**

贊成和反對

• 贊成 • ●●●●●●●●●●●●●●●●●●●

⤷Absolutely!
　絕對正確！

⤷Definitely!
　肯定是！

⤷You are exactly right!
　你說得太對了！

⤷That's exactly right!
　那對極了！

⤷I totally agree with what you say!
　我完全同意你所説的。

⤷That's exactly what I was thinking!
　那正是我所想的！

⤷There's no doubt about it.
　毫無疑問。

⤷That's my opinion, too.
　這也是我的意見。

⤷Well, I'm not completely sure, but I generally
　agree.
　哦，我沒有完全的把握，但我大體上同意。

反對

⇨You could be right, but don't you think that ...?
你可能是對的，但你是否認為……？

⇨Yes, that's true, but my feeling is that ...
那倒是真的，但我的感覺是……。

⇨I understand what you're saying, but in my opinion ...
我理解你所說的，但我的意見是……。

⇨I hate to disagree with you, but I believe ...
我不願和你有分歧，但我相信……。

⇨I'm afraid, I don't see it that way.
恐怕我不是那樣看的。

⇨I don't think so.
我不這麼認為。

⇨I don't agree with you.
我不同意你的看法。

⇨Are you joking?
你在開玩笑吧？

⇨I can't believe it.
我不感相信。

⮡You've got to be joking/kidding!
　你肯定是在開玩笑！

⮡That's absurd/ridiculous!
　這太荒謬/荒唐了！

實·用·會·話 1

A：Tom is a lovely boy.

B：Yes, I quite agree with you.

A：He never tells a lie.

B：Well, yes, that's quite true.

A：湯姆是個可愛的孩子。

B：是的。我很贊成。

A：他從不說謊。

B：噢，是的，很對。

深入分析

　1. agree with sb.意思是「同意某人的觀點或
　　意見」，例如：
　☑I can't agree with you.
　　我不同意你的觀點。
　☑Do you agree with me?

你同意我的提議嗎？

☑I agree with you on this point.

這一點我和你的意見一樣。

2. agree to do sth.意思是「同意某人去做某事」，例如：

☑She finally agreed to give up smoking.

她最終同意戒煙。

☑He has agreed to lend me money.

他已同意借我錢。

實·用·會·話 2

A：We're going to New York for summer vacation.

B：Sounds good.

A：Some people say it's a cool place in summer.

B：Well, I think they're right.

A：我們要去紐約度假了。

B：聽起來不錯呀。

A：有人說那兒夏天涼爽。

B：噢，我想他們是對的。

實·用·會·話 3

A：Our neighbor is very noisy.

B：No. I rather doubt that.

A：Why?

B：Because they're an old couple, and they go to bed very early at night.

A：我們的鄰居太吵了。

B：不，我很懷疑這一點。

A：為什麼？

B：因為他們是對老年夫婦，他們晚上都睡得很早。

 深入分析

doubt 在這裏用作動詞，意思是「懷疑、不相信、不確定」，例如：

☑They rather doubt that.

他們懷疑這一點。

☑I don't doubt that he will come.

我看他一定會來。

實·用·會·話 4

A：He is really a charming man.

B：Oh no, that's where I can't agree with
you.

A：What do you think of him then?

B：He's got a very bad temper.

A：他真是個很有趣的人。

B：哦，那正是我不贊成你的地方。

A：那你覺得他怎麼樣？

B：他脾氣很壞。

 深入分析

have got a very good/bad temper 意思是「脾
氣好（壞）」，例如：

☑As we all know, his father has got a very bad
temper.

眾所周知，他父親脾氣不好。

☑Her mother has got a very good temper.

她媽媽的脾氣很好。

實·用·會·話 5

A：Some say modern dances appeal to young people only.

B：I'm not sure I agree.

A：What makes you think that?

B：If you go to the city parks in the morning, you see hundreds of elderly people dancing disco.

A：Well, that is a modified form of disco.

B：True. But you also see lots of middle aged people in disco clubs in the evening.

A：I guess you are right.

A：有人說現代舞只有年輕人才喜歡。

B：我不太贊成這個說法。

A：為什麼不贊成？

B：如果你早晨去城市公園，你會看到成百上千的老年人在跳迪斯可。

A：哦，那是一種改良型的迪斯可。

B：說得對。在晚上，在迪斯可俱樂部，你也能

看到許多中年人。

A：我想你是對的。

深入分析

> appeal to 意思是「吸引、合胃口、引起共
> 鳴」，例如：
> ☑These painting appeal to me.
> 這些畫吸引了我。
> ☑This sort of music can't appeal to us.
> 這種音樂不能吸引我們。

實·用·會·話 6

A：My teacher told me that students should learn to think independently. Do you agree?

B：Definitely! Unfortunately, I don't think many teachers are teaching their students that way.

A：You are absolutely right.

B：You know what they should do? They should give us more opportunities to express our opinions and not be too strict

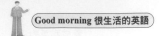
about what is correct or wrong.

A：That's a good idea.

A：我的老師告訴我說學生應該學會獨立思考。
　　你贊成嗎？

B：絕對贊成！不幸的是，我想，並不是許多老
　　師都是那樣來教導學生的。

A：你說的絕對正確。我認為老師們還是讓我們
　　去做太多的筆記和死記硬背的東西。

B：你知道他們該怎麼辦嗎？他們應給我們更多
　　的機會來表達我們的觀點，而且在對與錯的
　　問題上不要太嚴格。

A：這是個好主意。

深入分析

absolutely 意思是「完全地、絕對地」，例
如：

☑ What she said is absolutely right.

　她所說的完全正確。

☑ It's absolutely impossible.

　這絕對不可能。

☑ "So you decided to go with her?"

「所以你決定和她一起去？」

☑ "Absolutely"

「沒錯。」

實·用·會·話 7

A : By the way, how do you like the music they are playing?

B : It's pop music. Pop music isn't bad; but personally I prefer classical music.

A : Some say pop music is not pleasant to hear. Don't you think so?

B : I wouldn't say it's unpleasant. Pop music is exciting and stimulating.

A : But why do you like classical music more?

B : Well, it is only a matter of taste. Maybe I am a more conservative type of person.

A：你覺得他們演奏的音樂怎麼樣？

B：是流行樂。流行樂不錯，但我個人更喜歡古典音樂。

A：有人說流行音樂聽起來不舒服。你不這樣認為嗎？

B：我不會說不舒服。流行樂很能振奮人心。

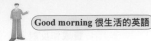

A：那你為什麼更喜歡古典音樂？

B：哦，這只是品味的問題。或許我是更保守類
　　型的人吧！

深入分析

> personally (speaking)意思是「就我個人而
> 言」，例如：
> ☑Personally, I like pop music better.
> 我個人更喜歡流行音樂。
> ☑Personally speaking, I agree with you
> 就個人而言，我同意的觀點。

實·用·會·話 8
────────────────────────

A：Some people say owning a private car is
　　too expensive. What's your opinion of it?

B：I'm not sure I can agree. I'd say cars are
　　very important means of transportation.

A：You still didn't convince me.

B：Well, only time will tell. You will see
　　more and more people driving their own
　　cars.

A：But what about the streets and traffic

jams?

B：Well, that's a different issue. You can't tell people not to buy cars simply because the streets are not wide enough, can you?

A：有人說擁有私人汽車是太過於昂貴的。你有什麼觀點？

B：我不這麼同意。我要說汽車是一種非常重要的交通工具。

A：你還沒有說服我。

B：噢，時間會證明一切。你會看到越來越多的人駕駛著他們自己的汽車。

A：但是街道和交通堵塞怎麼辦呢？

B：哦，這倒是個難解的問題。你不能單單因為街道不夠寬而叫人們不要買車，是吧？

 深入分析

convince 用作動詞，意思是「使某人信服、使明白」，例如：

☑I am convinced of his honesty.

我深信他的誠實。

☑All of us have been convinced that he is quite honest.

我們大家都相信他是十分誠實的。

實·用·會·話 9

A：Hello, Jim. I heard you have a new secretary.

B：Yeah, for only two weeks. Her name is Mary.

A：What do you think of her?

B：So far she has been doing OK.

A：Just OK?

B：Well, to be fair, more than OK. It's though still too early to tell.

　　She is very familiar with office routine, such as typing, filling, and taking phone calls.

A：How about her as a person, say, her manner and personality?

B：Oh, she is a very pleasant lady. She speaks softly and politely.

She is very patient with our clients and very helpful with colleagues.

A : How do you like her dress and makeup?

B : Wait a second. Why do you want to know so many details about her?

A : Well, to tell you the truth, Mary is my younger sister.

A : 喂，吉姆，聽說你有了個新秘書。

B : 是啊，有兩個星期了。她叫瑪麗。

A : 你認為她怎麼樣？

B : 到目前她表現得還不錯。

A : 只是還不錯？

B : 哦，坦白地說，比還不錯要好些，儘管現在下結論還尚早。她非常熟悉辦公室日常工作，例如打字、填表、接電話。

A : 她為人如何？例如舉止和個性？

B : 噢，她是個非常爽快的人。說話輕柔有禮，耐心對待客戶，對同事也很有幫助。

A : 她的服飾和打扮怎麼樣？

B : 等一下，為什麼你想瞭解這麼多關於她的細節？

A：哦，告訴你實話吧，瑪麗是我妹妹。

深入分析

1. be familiar with 意思是「對什麼很熟悉或很瞭解」，例如：

☑ I'm quite familiar with him.

　我對他很瞭解。

☑ Are you familiar with Miss Green?

　你對格林小姐很熟悉嗎？

2. so far 意思是「到目前為止」，用於完成時態中，例如：

☑ So far we have learned over 4,000 English words.

　到目前為止，我們已學了四千多個英語單字。

☑ So far they haven't heard of it.

　到目前為止，他們還沒有聽說此事。

拜訪

⮡Will it be all right to visit you tonight?
今晚我可以拜訪你嗎？

⮡Do you mind if I call on you this evening?
今晚我去拜訪你，你介意嗎？

⮡What time will it be all right?
什麼時間合適呢？

⮡I'd be happy if you could come.
你能來我將很高興。

⮡I'll be expecting you at home.
我會在家等你。

⮡It's very nice of you to come.
你能來真是太好了。

⮡How about some coffee?
來點咖啡如何？

⮡Would you like something to drink?
你想喝點什麼嗎？

⮡What would you like to drink, tea or coffee?
你想喝什麼，茶還是咖啡？

⮡Please don't bother.
別麻煩了。

Coffee, please.
請來點咖啡。

Do you have any cold drink, please?
請問你有什麼冷飲嗎？

Make yourself at home.
請自便。

Well, I'm afraid I must be leaving now.
噢，我想我得走了。

I really have to go.
我必須走了。

It's getting late.
時候不早了。

I've had a wonderful evening.
今晚過得很愉快。

It's been very nice talking to you.
和你談話真是太好了。

Thank you for coming.
謝謝你能來。

Thank you for your time.
感謝撥冗。

實·用·會·話 1

A : Oh, it's you. I've been expecting you.

B : Glad to see you. May I come in?

A : Sorry, I'm so happy that I forget to let you in. Please. I miss you very much.

B : Same with me. So I must come here.

A : Tea or coffee?

B : Tea, please. How things go recently?

A : Just fine. How about you?

B : Just so-so. I hear that you'll direct a new film. Is that true?

A : Yes, that's true.

B : That's great! I'm sure you'll make a great success.

A：噢，是你。我一直在等你。

B：見到你很高興。我能進來嗎？

A：對不起，我都高興得忘了讓你進來了。快請。我很想念你啊！

B：我也是。所以我一定得來。

A：喝茶還是咖啡？

B：請來點茶。最近怎麼樣？

A：還好。你呢？

B：馬馬虎虎。我聽說你將導演一部新片子。是真的嗎？

A：是真的。

B：太棒了！我肯定你會獲得成功的。

 深入分析

How things go recently?意思是「近來如何？」通常是朋友之間的寒暄之詞，以示關心，例如：

☑ I haven't seen you for several days. How things go recently?

好幾天沒見你了。近來如何？

☑ "How things go recently?"

「近來進展如何？」

"Not too bad."

「還不錯。」

實·用·會·話 2

A : Excuse me, Prof. Smith. I have some questions to discuss with you. I wonder if it will be all right to visit you in the afternoon.

B：I'd be happy if you could come, but this afternoon is all booked up. What about tomorrow afternoon?

A：Well, I have classes tomorrow afternoon.

B：Maybe you can come to my house this evening.

A：What time will it be all right?

B：How about 8 o'clock after I have my dinner?

A：That's fine.

B：All right then. I'll be expecting you.

(In the evening)

A：Is Prof. Smith in?

B：Hi, come on in. Make yourself at home. Can I fetch you some thing to drink, coffee or tea?

A：Tea, please.

A：對不起，史密斯教授。我有幾個問題想和你討論一下。不知道今天下午拜訪您是否合

適。

B：你能來我很高興，但今天下午行程排滿了。
　　明天下午怎麼樣？

A：哦，明天下午我有課。

B：或許今天晚上你可以到我家來。

A：幾點鐘方便呢？

B：我吃過晚飯後，八點怎麼樣？

A：好的。

B：那好，我等你啊。

（晚上）

A：史密斯教授在嗎？

B：嗨！進來吧。請不要拘束啊。我給你弄點喝
　　的，咖啡還是茶？

A：請來點茶吧。

 深入分析

　1. be booked up 意思是「已滿座、時間已排
　　　滿」，例如：

　☑This week is booked up.

　　　這週時間已排滿了。

　☑The theater is booked up.

　　　劇院 (座位) 已坐滿了。

2. make sb. at home 意思是「使某人感覺如在家中、使某人自在、不要拘束」的意思，例如：

☑What he said made me at home.

他的話使我很自在。

☑Please make yourself at home.

請不要拘束。

實·用·會·話 3

A：It's getting late. I'm afraid I must be leaving now.

B：Just stay a little bit longer.

A：I would like to but I have to be going. I had a good time today.

Thank you for everything.

B：You're welcome. I'm glad you like it.

A：Good night.

B：Good night.

A：不早了。我想我得走了。

B：再多待一會兒吧。

A：我是想啊，可是我必須走了。今天過得很愉快。謝謝你所做的一切。

B：別客氣。我很高興你能喜歡。

A：晚安。

B：晚安。

 深入分析

> I would like to 意思是「我想……」，通常
> 可縮寫為 I'd like to，例如：
> ☑I'd like to have a cup of tea.
>   我想喝杯茶。
> ☑I'd like to have a swim.
>   我想游泳。
> ☑ "Would you like to go to a movie with
>   me?"
>   「你今晚想和我一起去看電影嗎？」
>   "I'd like to but I can't."
>   「我很想去，但是我不能去。」

實·用·會·話 4

A：I'm very sorry, but I won't be able to come over to your new house tomorrow morning. I have to meet a friend at the airport.

B：That's all right. We can make it some other time. Suppose we can meet next Sunday.

A：Fine. I'll call you then.

B：OK. So long.

A：很抱歉，明天早上我不能到你的新房子來了。我得去機場接一位朋友。

B：沒關係。我們可以另約時間。我提議下個星期天怎麼樣。

A：好的。到時我打電話給你。

B：好吧。再見。

 深入分析

suppose 用於句首，構成祈使句，表示提出建議，意思是「提議……」，例如：

☑Suppose we go for a swim.

我提議我們去游泳。

☑Suppose we can go and ask him for some advice.

我提議我們可以去向他尋求一些建議。

實·用·會·話 5

A : Good morning, Prof. Brown.

B : Oh, it's David. Glad to meet you in my house.

A : Glad to meet you, too. Nice day, isn't it?

B : Yes, a nice day. Let me get you something to drink, tea or coffee?

A : Just water, please. I wonder if you could tell me how to improve my oral English.

B : If you want to improve it in a short time, there is only one way, that's you must speak English at any time you can.

A : Yes, I know. But in what way?

B : For example, you can speak English in class and talk with your classmates or discuss something with your teacher.

A : I see.

B : You can also listen to the radio or watch TV.

A : OK. I'll practice it from tonight on.

B : I'm sure you can speak very well some-
day.

A : I hope so. I'm sorry, I must go now.
Thank you very much.

B : Not at all. Thank you for your coming.
Good-bye.

A：早安，伯朗教授。

B：噢，是大衛啊。很高興能在我家裏見到你。

A：見到你我也很高興。天氣不錯，是吧？

B：是啊，一個好天氣。我給你弄點喝的，茶還
是咖啡？

A：喝水就好。您能否給我建議怎樣提高我的英
語口語能力。

B：如果你想在短期內提高口語表達能力，只有
一個可行的辦法，那就是利用一切機會說英
語。

A：是的，我知道了。但怎麼去說呢？

B：例如，你可以在班上說英語，和你的同學講
話或和老師討論問題時也說英語。

A：我知道了。

B：你還可以聽收音機或看電視。

A：好，我將從今晚開始練習。

B：我相信有一天，你的英語能說得很好。

A：我也希望如此。很抱歉，我該走了。非常感謝。

B：別客氣。謝謝你的光臨。再見。

 深入分析

　　for example「舉例來說」，這是一句非常實用的口語化英文，當你要解釋你的觀念或見解時，需要有例子佐證，此時就適合在句首說 for example,...。類似的用法也可以說 for instance。

☑For example, go see a doctor. Maybe it will help.

　　例如去看醫生吧！也許會有幫助。

實·用·會·話 6

A：Good morning, Mr. Brown. May I come in?

B：Certainly you can. Come in, please.

A：Not a bad day!

B：Yes. What would you like to drink?

A : A cup of tea, please. I often heard Peter mention you when I was in Taiwan. He asked me to visit you when I came to America.

B : Thanks. How about things going with Peter?

A : Very good. He is studying in Taiwan University and misses you very much. How about you recently?

B : Not bad, I have a book published recently.

A : Congratulate you! You are always good.

B : Thank you.

A : It's too late now. I think I should go now.

B : Remember me to Peter when you meet him. Good-bye.

A : 早安，布朗先生。 我可以進來嗎？

B : 當然可以。請進。

A : 今天天氣不錯！

B : 是啊。喝點什麼？

A : 來杯茶吧。我在台灣時常聽彼得談起你，我

來美國的時候他請我來看看你。

B：謝謝。彼得過得怎麼樣？

A：很好。他在台灣大學讀書，時常想念你。你最近過得好嗎？

B：還不錯，最近出了一本書。

A：恭喜你！你一直都很棒。

B：謝謝。

A：時間不早了。我該走了。

B：見到彼得代我向他問好。再見。

深入分析

1. How about things going?意思是「事情進展如何？」，例如：

☑ "How about things going?"

「一切進展如何？」

"Not too bad."

「還不錯。」

2. remember sb. to sb. else 意思是「代某人向他人問好」，例如：

☑ Please remember me to your parents.

請代我向你的父母問好。

☑ Please remember me to your family.

請代我向你的家人問好。

Unit 19

邀請

•問句•

▷How about having dinner with me tonight?
要不要今晚和我一起吃飯？

▷Would you like to see the new film?
你想去看這部新片子嗎？

▷Are you going to be busy this evening?
今晚忙嗎？

▷Do you have any plans next Sunday?
你下個星期天有任何計劃嗎？

▷I was wondering if you would like to go to the movie with me.
不知道你是不是想和我去看電影。

▷I wonder if you would be free this afternoon.
不知道你今天下午是否有空。

▷What time would be convenient for you?
什麼時間對你合適？

▷Would Tuesday morning suit you?
星期二早晨對你合適嗎？

▷What about Friday afternoon?

星期五下午怎麼樣？

⇨How would ten-thirty be?
十點半如何？

•回答•••••••••••••••••••••••••••

⇨I'd love to.
我願意。

⇨That's a great idea.
好主意。

⇨That sounds great.
聽起來不錯。

⇨I'll be free tomorrow afternoon.
明天下午我有空。

⇨I'm sorry, but Tuesday won't be so convenient
for me.
對不起，但星期二我不太方便。

⇨I'm afraid I can't make it today.
今天恐怕不行。

⇨I'm afraid tonight is a bit of problem.
恐怕今晚有點問題。

實·用·會·話 1

A：Are you free this evening, Jim?

B：Yes. Why?

A：Do you feel like going to that new kara-oke?

B：Oh, that's a good idea.

A：今晚有空嗎，吉姆？

B：有啊。怎麼了？

A：你想去那一家新開張的卡拉OK店嗎？

B：噢，好主意。

深入分析

　　feel like 意思是「想要去做某事嗎？」，
例如：

☑Do you feel like having a cup of coffee?

　　你想喝杯咖啡嗎？

☑We'll go for a walk, if you feel like it.

　　如果你願意，我們去散散步。

實·用·會·話 2

A : Jim, are you doing anything special this weekend?

B : Yes. Peter and I have promised to call on a new customer.

A : Oh, well, never mind. But I was thinking of asking you and your wife to go out for dinner.

B : That sounds great. I wonder if we could make it some other time.

A : How about Sunday evening, at seven o'clock?

B : That'll be all right. See you then.

A：古姆，本週末有什麼事嗎？

B：有。彼得和我答應過去拜訪一位新顧客。

A：哦，那沒關係。我想請你和你太太一起出去吃飯。

B：那好啊。要不要另外約個時間？

A：星期天晚上，七點鐘？

B：好的。到時見。

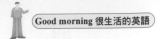
深入分析

call on 意思是「拜訪」，常用句型為 call on sd.，例如：

☑Tomorrow we'll call on Prof. Smith.

明天我們將拜訪史密斯教授。

☑When are you going to call on your teacher?

你打算何時拜訪你的老師？

實·用·會·話 3

(On the phone)

A：Dr. Anderson's office. May I help you?

B：Yes. I'd like to make an appointment for a physical checkup.

A：Are you a regular patient?

B：No, I'm not. I recently moved to this area.

A：I see. I I'm afraid Dr. Anderson I can't see you this week. Will next Monday morning be all right?

B：OK. What time would you like me to come? Suppose I come at 8?

A：Good. We'll see you then.

（電話中）

A：安德森醫生辦公室。我能幫你做什麼？

B：我想約個時間，做個體檢。

A：你是定期病人嗎？

B：不是。我最近剛搬到這個地區。

A：我明白了。恐怕這週安德森醫生我不能見你。下週一早上怎麼樣？

B：好的。我幾點來呢？八點？

A：好。就八點吧。

深入分析

    make an appointment 意思是「與某人約會」，通常是正式的會面，而非情侶間的「約會」（date）例如：

☑ I've an appointment with my dentist at 3 pm.
我已約定下午三點去看牙醫。

☑ Do you want to make an appointment for a physical examination?
你想約個時間，做個體檢嗎？

實·用·會·話 4

A : Oh, Mr. Brown, I'm sorry, I won't be able to keep my appointment with you for Thursday. You see, I have to fly to Hong Kong this afternoon on urgent business. Could we postpone our meeting to sometime early next week?

B : Certainly. What about Monday morning?

A : That would be fine. Shall we make it nine o'clock?

B : All right.

A : I'm very sorry about Thursday.

B : Oh, that's quite all right. I understand perfectly.

A : 哦，伯朗先生，對不起，我們星期四的約會我不能赴約了。今天下午因有急事得飛往香港。我們能把約會延到下週早些時候嗎？

B : 當然可以。星期一早上怎麼樣？

A : 好的，我們約在九點吧？

B：好吧。

A：星期四的事我很抱歉。

B：哦，沒關係，我完全理解。

 深入分析

　　keep one's appointment 意思是「實踐約定、遵守諾言」，例如：

☑I think you should keep your appointment.

　　我想你應該遵守諾言。

☑Today I'm so tired that maybe I won't be able to keep my appointment.

　　今天我太累了，也許我得失約了。

實·用·會·話 5

A : When can we expect you for dinner? Can you come tonight?

B : Not tonight. I promised to go to a concert with my sister.

A : Well, how about Friday then?

B : That sounds fine.

A : Good. Shall we say seven o'clock?

B : I'll be there.

A：什麼時候我們能請你吃晚飯？今晚你能來嗎？

B：今晚不行。我答應過我妹妹一起去參加音樂會。

A：那麼，星期五行嗎？

B：好吧。

A：好。我們約在七點吧？

B：我會準時到的。

 深入分析

　　how about...意思是「……怎麼樣？」，可以接名詞或動名詞式子句，例如：

☑How about today?

　今天行嗎？

☑How about this pair of shoes?

　這雙鞋子怎麼樣？

☑How about having a dinner with me?

　和我吃晚餐如何？

實·用·會·話 6

(On the phone)

A：Hello! May I speak to Mr. Smith, please?

B：This is John Smith speaking.

A：Good morning, Mr. Smith. This is Mary speaking. I'm very sorry to say I have to put off our appointment for this afternoon from three to five, because something urgent has just come up.

B：I'm afraid I have another appointment at five. How about tomorrow afternoon? Would that be too late?

A：No. That'll be all right. When will it be convenient for you?

B：How about two?

A：All right. I'm sorry about this change. See you tomorrow.

B：See you then.

（電話中）

A：喂！我可以與史密斯先生通話嗎？

B：我就是約翰‧史密斯。

A：早安，史密斯先生。我是瑪麗呀。很抱歉，因為有急事，我得將我們今天下午的約會從三點延到五點。

B：我五點另有約會呀。明天下午怎麼樣？那樣
　　會太晚嗎？

A：可以，不晚。你幾點鐘方便？

B：兩點怎麼樣？

A：好啊！我很抱歉這次改變時間。明天見。

B：到時見。

 深入分析

1. put off 意思是「延遲」，例如：

☑The event was put off because of a rain.
　　活動因天雨而延遲。

☑The meeting will be put off till tomorrow.
　　會議將延遲至明天。

2. come up 意思是「出現、發生」，例如：

☑I don't know when it came up.
　　我不知道那是何時發生的？

☑A stranger suddenly came up.
　　突然一個陌生人出現了。

1. What kind of clothes lasts the longest?

   什麼衣服穿得最久？

2. Why are farmers cruel?

   為什麼農夫是殘酷的？

英語腦筋急轉彎 ．．．．解答

1. Underwear, because it's never worn out.

   是內衣，因為它永遠不會穿在外面。

   原來如此

   worn 為穿著 wear 的過去式，又表示「磨損」的意思。

2. They pull corns by ears.

   因為他們揪著玉米耳朵摘玉米。

   原來如此

   ear 除了耳朵的意思之外，也表示玉蜀黍的穗。

Unit **20**

看醫生

•問句• •

⇨What's wrong with you/your leg?
　你怎麼了？/你的腿怎麼了？

⇨What's the matter with you?
　你怎麼了？

⇨What seems to be the trouble?
　怎麼回事？

⇨Aren't you feeling well?
　你感覺不舒服嗎？

⇨How long have you been like this?
　你像這樣有多長時間了？

⇨How long have you had it?
　你有這症狀多長時間了？

⇨Since when have you been feeling like this?
　從什麼時候起有這種感覺的？

⇨How long has this been going on?
　像這樣有多長時間了？

⇨Can you bend over and touch your toes?
　你可以彎腰摸到你的腳指嗎？

⇨What happened to you?
發生什麼事了？

⇨When did it happen?
什麼時候發生的？

⇨Your blood pressure is down.
你的血壓很低。

⇨You should lose some weight.
你應該要減肥。

⇨Try to eat less fat and salt.
試著少吃脂肪和鹽巴。

⇨How often do you exercise?
你多久運動？

⇨How do you feel today?
你今天覺得如何？

•結論• ● ● ● ● ● ● ● ● ● ● ● ● ● ● ● ● ● ● ●

⇨Nothing serious.
沒什麼嚴重。

⇨It's just a cold. There is nothing to worry about.
只是感冒，沒什麼好擔心的。

▷You have to stop smoking/drinking.
　你得戒煙/戒酒。

▷You should stay in bed for a couple of days.
　你應該臥床幾天。

▷Have a good rest.
　好好休息。

▷Stay in bed for a few days.
　在床上多休息幾天。

▷You can take aspirin for your headache.
　頭痛可以吃阿司匹靈。

▷You should get some rest.
　你應該要多休息。

▷It's nothing serious, but you'd better stay in bed for a day for two.
　沒什麼大不了的，但你最好臥床休息一兩天。

說明症狀 ● ● ● ● ● ● ● ● ● ● ● ● ● ● ● ● ● ● ●

▷I've got a high fever and I feel dizzy.
　我發高燒而且眩暈。

▷I seem to be catching a cold.

我好像感冒了。

➪I think I'm coming down with the flu.
我想我感染了流感。

➪I don't feel well.
我感覺不好。

➪I really feel awful.
我覺得很糟糕。

➪I woke up with a terrible headache and I have a fever.
我起床後頭很痛,而且我發燒了。

➪My throat hurts, too.
我的喉嚨也很痛。

➪My throat\shoulder\arm\hand\leg\ foot hurts.
我的喉嚨\肩膀\手臂\腿\腳痛。

➪But my back still hurts.
可是我的背還是很痛。

➪I cut my finger on Sunday, but the cut wasn't too bad.
我星期天切到手,但是不嚴重。

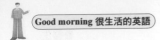

⮕I put on a bandage at home.
我在家裡有綁繃帶。

⮕Should I change my diet?
我需要注意飲食嗎？

實·用·會·話 1

A：What's the trouble?

B：I've got a sore throat and my chest hurts, and I feel a bit dizz.

A：How long have you been like this?

B：Two or three days.

A：Do you have a headache?

B：Yes, I do. And I think I've got a fever, too.

A：Do you sneeze?

B：Yes.

A：Let me take your temperature and listen to your lungs. Well, I think you've caught the flu.

B：What do you advise, doctor?

A：Take this prescription to the drugstore

for the medicine.

B：How should I take the medicine?

A：Take one big tablet and two small ones three times a day after meals.

Furthermore, there is nothing better for you than plenty of water and sleep.

A：怎麼了？

B：我喉嚨疼，胸部也疼，感覺有點頭暈。

A：有多長時間了？

B：兩三天了。

A：頭疼嗎？

B：有。我想我也有發燒。

A：打噴嚏嗎？

B：有。

A：我給你量量體溫，聽聽你的肺部。哦，我想你是得了流感。

B：你有什麼建議，醫生？

A：把這個藥方拿到藥房去取藥。

B：藥怎麼服用呢？

A：大的一片，小的兩片，一日三次，飯後服用。

還有，你最好多多喝水，充足睡眠。

1. What's the trouble with...? /What's the matter with...?意思是「……怎麼了？」是醫生看診時一種非常實用句型，例如：

☑ "What's the trouble with you?"
   「你怎麼了？」
   "I have got a cold."
   「我感冒了。」

2. take one's temperature 意思是「給某人量體溫」，例如：

☑ The doctor is going to take his temperature.
   醫生將給他量體溫。

☑ Have you taken your son's temperature?
   你給你兒子量過體溫了嗎？

實·用·會·話 2

A：What is the matter with you?

B：I have a terrible toothache.

A：Which tooth is it?

B：This one here.

A：Ah, yes. There's a cavity.

B：Can you fill it?

A : I'm afraid not. It's too late. It'll have to be taken out.

B : Then I want to have it taken out now.

A : You'd better wait. The gums are swollen. Take the medicine I give and come back in three days.

A：你怎麼不舒服？

B：我的牙疼得厲害。

A：哪一顆牙？

B：這邊的這顆。

A：啊，是的。有一個洞。

B：你能把它補上嗎？

A：恐怕不能，太遲了。必須把它拔掉。

B：那我想現在就拔掉。

A：你最好等一等。牙床有點腫。服用我給你開的藥，三天後再來。

深入分析

> take out 意思是「取出、拿出」，例如：
>
> ☑Please take out your book and turn to page 6.
> 請取出書並翻到第六頁。

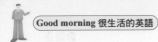

☑He took out several books from the drawer.

他從抽屜裏拿出幾本書。

實·用·會·話 3

A : What's the matter with you? Are you hurt?

B : I slipped on the icy road and fell down. I think my arm is broken.

A : Oh! Which arm is it?

B : The right one. It hurts right here.

A : Let me see. You'd better have an X-ray.

B : Is it serious?

A : I'm not sure. Wait until we get the report from the lab.

A：你怎麼了？受傷了嗎？

B：我在結冰的路上滑了一下，摔倒了。我想我的胳膊斷了。

A：噢，哪一隻胳膊？

B：右臂。就這兒疼。

A：我瞧瞧。你最好拍一張X光片。

B：嚴重嗎？

A：我不敢肯定。等攝影室的報告吧。

深入分析

sb. had better do……意思是「最好做……」
可寫為 sb. 'd better do...，是建議某人做某事
之意如：

☑You'd better have a rest.

你最好休息一下。

☑You'd better give up the foolish idea.

你最好放棄這愚蠢的想法。

實·用·會·話 4

A：Is it serious, doctor?

B：No, just a bad cold.

A：I hope it won't last long.

B：It shouldn't if you take good care of yourself. Take the medicine I've prescribed and get plenty of rest.

A：Do I have to go on a diet?

B：It's not necessary. Drink plenty of water and since your stomach is upset, avoid eating much oily food.

A：嚴重嗎，醫生？

B：不嚴重，只是重感冒。

A：我希望不會持續太長時間。

B：好好照顧自己，病情就不會持續太久。服用我給你開的藥，多多休息。

A：我要吃規定的飲食嗎？

B：不必要。多喝水，既然你胃不舒服，就避免吃太多油膩的食物。

深入分析

go on a diet 是「吃規定的飲食（節食）」，也可以用 be on a diet 表示，例如：

☑The doctor asked me to go on a diet, for I was too fat.

醫生讓我吃規定的飲食，因為我太胖了。

☑I think the fat should go on a diet.

我認為肥胖的人應該節食。

☑I am on a diet now.

我現在正在節食中。

實·用·會·話 5

A：Doctor, whenever I cough I have a burning sensation in my throat and my chest hurts.

B：Are you coughing up phlegm?

A：Yes, and it smells terrible.

B：I hear a wheezing sound. Do you have difficulty breathing?

A：Yes, I do.

B：How long have you had a fever?

A：About a week.

A：醫生，每當我咳嗽時，（喉嚨）就有灼痛的感覺，而且胸部也會痛。

B：你有沒有咳出痰來？

A：有，而且很難聞。

B：我聽到哮喘的聲音。你有沒有呼吸困難的現象？

A：有。

B：你發燒多久了？

A：大約一個星期。

深入分析

　　have difficulty (in) doing sth.意思是「做某事有困難」，例如：

☑Do you think you still have any difficulty in spelling?

你認為你在拼字方面還有困難嗎？

☑I have difficulty in speaking English fluently.

我無法說流利的英語。

☑I have no difficulty working out this problem.

我毫不費力地算出這道題。

實·用·會·話 6

A：I feel quite sick, doctor.

B：What symptoms do you have?

A：I have a runny nose and can't stop coughing.

B：Do you have a fever?

A：I took my temperature just before I left home, and it was 38.5℃.

B：Have you been vomiting?

A：No, I haven't.

B：Well, you should rest for two or three days. I'll prescribe some medicine.

A：Thank you.

A：我病得很重，醫生。

B：你有什麼症狀？

A：我流鼻涕而且不停地咳嗽。

B：有沒有發燒？

A：我離家之前量過體溫，攝氏三十八度半。

B：有沒有嘔吐？

A：沒有。

B：噢，你應該休息兩三天，我會開些藥給你。

A：謝謝。

 深入分析

1. prescribe 意思是「開（藥方）」，例如：
   ☑ The doctor has prescribed some medicines
   for the little girl.
   醫生已為小女孩開了一些藥。
   ☑ What do you prescribe for this illness?
   你對此病開什麼藥方？
2. runny nose 是「鼻子流鼻水」的意思，可
   別誤會為「會跑動的鼻子」。

稱讚他人

・稱讚・ ●●●●●●●●●●●●●●●●●●●●●●●●●●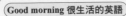

➪You are looking fine.
　你看起來很好。

➪You don't look your age.
　你看起來比實際年齡年輕。

➪You've lost some weight.
　你瘦了。

➪You've done a good job.
　做得不錯。

➪I can't believe my eyes!
　我真不相信我所看到的！

➪How nice!
　太好了！

➪Wonderful!
　妙極了！

➪What a beautiful sweater!
　好漂亮的毛線衫！

➪What a pretty necklace!
　好美的項鍊！

➪Your tie looks good on you.
你的領帶很適合你。

➪That dress looks great on you.
你穿那衣服看起來很棒。

➪You look great in that new dress.
你穿那新衣服看起來很棒。

➪Your blouse goes beautifully with that skirt.
你的襯衫配那裙子很好看。

➪Your belt goes just right with your blue pants.
你的腰帶正好配那條藍色褲子。

➪It looks smart.
看起來很棒。

➪That's absolutely super.
那絕對是出色。

➪You look smart/beautiful/handsome today.
你今天看起來很棒/美麗/瀟灑。

➪That's a smart car.
那是輛很棒的車。

⇨Thank you. It's very nice of you to say so.
謝謝你。你能這麼説真是好。

⇨Thank you very much for saying so.
非常感謝你這麼説。

⇨I'm flattered.
受寵若驚。

⇨You flatter me.
你恭維我。

⇨I'm glad you like it.
我很高興你喜歡。

⇨Thank you. And yours is nice, too.
謝謝。你的也很不錯。

⇨Thank you for the compliment.
多謝讚美。

實·用·會·話 1

A：How do you like this tie?

B：It looks good on you.

A：What about the color?

B：It's nice.

A：Isn't it too bright?

B：No, it's perfect. It goes well with that suit.

A：你覺得這個領帶怎麼樣？

B：你打著（這條領帶）看起來不錯。

A：顏色呢？

B：不錯呀。

A：不會太亮嗎？

B：不，很完美。和那套西服配起來很好。

 深入分析

"go well with"不是「一起去」的意思，在此處是「和……搭配得很好」的意思，例如：

☑I like this tie because it goes well with my suit.

我喜歡這條領帶，因為它和我的西服搭配得很好。

☑They don't think the pair of shoes goes well with my dress.

他們認為這雙鞋子和我的裙子搭配得不好。

實·用·會·話 2

A : That's a marvelous jacket.

B : Does it really look OK?

A : Yes, and I like the color and design, too.
It matches your pants well.

B : I got it on sale when I was in Taipei last
month.

A : You were lucky to get it.

A：那是件極棒的上衣。

B：看起來還真的不錯嗎？

A：是的，而且我也喜歡這顏色和款式。和你的
褲子很相配。

B：這是我上個月在台北大減價時買的。

A：你可真走運。

深入分析

"match"除了有「比賽」、「較量」的意思
外，還表示「相當」、「相配」，表示兩者
之間的協調性相當高，例如：

☑The carpets should match the curtains.

地毯該和窗簾相配。

☑She was wearing a brown dress with hat and gloves to match.

她穿著一件棕色的衣服，並有帽子和手套相配。

☑The color of the shirt does not match that of the tie.

襯衫的顏色與領帶不相配。

實·用·會·話 3

A : Hi, Lena. You look great tonight!

B : Thank you. By the way, you look terrific with your new tie.

A : Do I? Thanks. Your dress is really beautiful.

B : It's a present from my boy friend.

A：嗨，林娜。你今晚看起來真漂亮！

B：謝謝。對了，你繫的領帶看起來很棒。

A：是嗎？謝謝。你的衣服真漂亮。

B：是我男友給我的禮物。

實·用·會·話 4

A : Sophia, you really can sing, can't you?

B : Thanks, Mark. I used to be a member of the school choir.

A : No wonder you can control your voice so well. You are a professional singer.

B : Well, I wouldn't say I am a professional, but I did receive some training at school. My music teacher used to be a professional singer.

A : Well, a good teacher makes good students.

B : You got this one right.

A : 蘇菲亞，你唱得真不賴，不是嗎？

B : 多謝，馬克。我過去是學校樂團的成員。

A : 怪不得你的嗓音控制得這麼好，原來你是個職業歌手呀。

B : 噢，我可不敢說是個職業歌手，但在學校我確實受過一些訓練。我的音樂老師曾經是位職業歌手。

A : 哦，名師出高徒啊。

B : 這話你說得對。

深入分析

"no wonder" 意思是「毫不奇怪」、「難怪」,表示先前猜測或評論是符合預期的,例如:

☑No wonder she will like this color.

難怪她會喜歡這顏色。

☑No wonder he can win the game.

難怪他能贏得這場比賽。

實·用·會·話 5

A：I love your shirt.

B：Do you really like it?

A：Yes, it fits perfectly.

B：It's pure silk, but it wasn't very expensive.

A：That's amazing. It certainly looks expensive.

A：我喜歡你的襯衫。

B：你真的喜歡嗎?

A：真的。(這件穿起來)非常合身。

B：是純絲的,但並不是太貴。

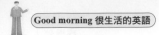

A：太不可思議了。看起來很名貴的呀！

實·用·會·話 6

A：What do you think of my new hat?

B：It's very nice. It goes beautifully with your dress.

A：Thank you. It's very nice of you to say so.

B：You're welcome.

A：My sister gave me this hat for my birth-day.

B：She has excellent taste.

A：你認為我的新帽子怎麼樣？

B：很好的，配你的衣服很好看。

A：謝謝。你這樣說真是太好了。

B：別客氣。

A：這是我生日時，我姐姐送我的帽子。

B：她的品味極好。

深入分析

"taste"除了是「味道」的意思之外,也可以表示「審美力」、「鑒賞力」,例如:

☑She has excellent taste in dress.

　她對衣著有極好的鑒賞力。

☑The lady dresses in perfect taste.

　這位女士穿著的品味極佳。

國家圖書館出版品預行編目資料

Good morning 很生活的英語／張瑜凌編著.

--初版.--臺北縣汐止市 ： 雅典文化,民 96

面；公分. --（全民學英文系列：4）

ISBN：978-986-7041-32-6（平裝）

1. 英國語言－會話

805.188   96001343

Good morning 很生活的英語

編　　著◎ 張瑜凌
出 版 者◎ 雅典文化事業有限公司
登 記 證◎ 局版北市業字第五七〇號
發 行 人◎ 黃玉雲
執行編輯◎ 張瑜凌
編 輯 部◎ 221 台北縣汐止市大同路三段 194–1 號 9 樓
　　　　　EmailAdd: a8823.a1899@msa.hinet.net
　　　　　電話◎02-86473663　傳真◎ 02-86473660
郵　　撥◎ 18965580 雅典文化事業有限公司
法律顧問◎ 永信法律事務所　林永頌律師
總 經 銷◎ 永續圖書有限公司
　　　　　221 台北縣汐止市大同路三段 194–1 號 9 樓
　　　　　EmailAdd: yungjiuh@ms45.hinet.net
　　　　　網站◎ www.foreverbooks.com.tw
　　　　　郵撥◎ 18669219
　　　　　電話◎ 02-86473663　傳真◎ 02-86473660
　　　　　ISBN：978-986-7041-32-6（平裝）
初　　版◎2007 年 4 月
定　　價◎ NT$ **149** 元

雅典文化 讀者回函卡

謝謝您購買這本書。

為加強對讀者的服務，請您詳細填寫本卡，寄回雅典文化；
並請務必留下您的E-mail帳號，我們會主動將最近 "好康"
的促銷活動告訴您，保證值回票價。

書　　　名：**Good morning 很生活的英語**

購買書店：＿＿＿＿＿市／縣＿＿＿＿＿＿＿書店

姓　　　名：＿＿＿＿＿＿＿　生　日：＿＿＿年＿＿月＿＿日

身分證字號：＿＿＿＿＿＿＿＿＿＿＿＿＿＿＿

電　　　話：(私)＿＿＿＿＿(公)＿＿＿＿＿(手機)＿＿＿＿＿

地　　　址：□□□

E - mail：＿＿＿＿＿＿＿＿＿＿＿＿＿＿＿

年　　　齡：□20歲以下　□21歲～30歲　□31歲～40歲
　　　　　　□41歲～50歲　□51歲以上

性　　　別：□男　□女　　婚姻：□單身　□已婚

職　　　業：□學生　　□大眾傳播　□自由業　□資訊業
　　　　　　□金融業　□銷售業　　□服務業　□教職
　　　　　　□軍警　　□製造業　　□公職　　□其他

教育程度：□高中以下（含高中）□大專　□研究所以上

職 位 別：□負責人　□高階主管　□中級主管
　　　　　□一般職員　□專業人員

職 務 別：□管理　　　□行銷　　□創意　　□人事、行政
　　　　　□財務、法務　　□生產　□工程　　□其他＿＿＿

您從何得知本書消息？
　□逛書店　　□報紙廣告　□親友介紹
　□出版書訊　□廣告信函　□廣播節目
　□電視節目　□銷售人員推薦
　□其他＿＿＿＿＿＿＿＿＿＿

您通常以何種方式購書？
　□逛書店　□劃撥郵購　□電話訂購　□傳真訂購　□信用卡
　□團體訂購　□網路書店　□其他＿＿＿＿＿

看完本書後，您喜歡本書的理由？
　□內容符合期待　□文筆流暢　□具實用性　□插圖生動
　□版面、字體安排適當　　□內容充實
　□其他＿＿＿＿＿＿＿＿＿＿

看完本書後，您不喜歡本書的理由？
　□內容不符合期待　□文筆欠佳　□內容平平
　□版面、圖片、字體不適合閱讀　　□觀念保守
　□其他＿＿＿＿＿＿＿＿＿＿

您的建議：
＿＿＿＿＿＿＿＿＿＿＿＿＿＿＿＿＿＿＿＿＿＿＿

廣 告 回 信
基隆郵局登記證
基隆廣字第 056 號

22103

台北縣汐止市大同路三段 194 號 9 樓之 1

雅典文化事業有限公司

編輯部　收

請沿此虛線對折免貼郵票，以膠帶黏貼後寄回，謝謝！

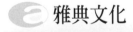

雅典文化

為你開啟知識之殿堂